BLOOD RITUALS

A.J. SOIFER

undercover BOOKS

PRELUDE

FRIDAY, FEBRUARY 4

T he night the Wainstein family was to die was like any other Friday night, with family members preparing to greet Shabbat. But, for little Sharon, it didn't feel like any other Shabbat night.

Chaia assisted her daughter in lighting the final ceremonial candle before turning to face his husband. He didn't notice the look from her wife as he was praying, whispering Hebrew words at full speed with his eyes closed. His body swung, accompanying his words, bringing the brim of his shtreimel, the all-black fur hat he wore, closer to the wall at every swing he took.

"Mommy, I am hungry! Can we start dinner already?"

Chaia took his index finger to his closed lips, signaling her daughter to keep it quiet.

The girl was feeling a little annoyed and bored. Her day had been long. Because it was Friday, she was let out of school early to help her mom prepare for the weekend celebration. It was only eleven o'clock in the morning when she returned home. Her mother made her help with all the preparations for the special night and caring for her younger brother, Mendel.

Her father had come home earlier that day, shortly after she got home from school. Sharon was a young girl, but she had lived long enough to know that his father would only come home after praying in the temple on Fridays. And that would never be before nine. There was also that tall cross in the middle of the living room his father had spent the entire afternoon putting together. She had seen nothing like that before. When she tried to ask her mother about the cross, Chaia shooed her dismissively.

She was bored. Annoyed and bored and now also hungry.

Chaia, noticing her daughter's growing impatience, told her to take care of his brother and bring him to the table just as they were about to begin dinner.

The man stopped praying. He took a deep breath and then declared that it was time. Chaia agreed and went to their back-of-the-house bedroom.

The man wiped his brow and checked that his black tie was perfectly aligned at the center of his clean white dress shirt.

Chaia came returned carrying something green in her hands. Sharon felt curious about that and tried to take it from her mother's hands, but then his father gave her the penetrating glance he gave her every time he was angry, and she backed off. Chaia put the green thing on the dinner table, and Sharon tried to touch it. She quickly pulled her hands away when she saw it was sharp and pointy. She looked at it with interest.

"What is this, Mommy?" she asked.

"Just be quiet," Chaia answered.

The little girl tried to get help from his father, who responded with an assertive silence and a severe and grim face.

"Take your seat at the table."

The women complied, taking seats on his right.

The man served a cup of wine until it overflew, making a blood-like stain on the cloth. He prayed before taking the cup in his hand, taking a sip, and passing it to his wife, who also took a sip. Then, the man said it was time for the ceremonial wash of hands. The whole family got up and went into the kitchen. The husband and wife threw water at each other's hands using a jar with two handles. When they finished, Chaia helped her daughter and son do the same.

Sharon experienced the same annoyance she had been experiencing all day. Something was off. She felt there was a lack of joy in the room. After the ceremonial hand washing, the father invited them back to the table. He uncovered the two loaves of ceremonial bread, the challah, in a silver plate and recited: "*Baruch atah, Adonai Eloheinu, Melech haolam, haMotzi lechem min haaretz.*" When he finished, his wife and daughter said, "Amen." Then, he took one piece out of the loaf of bread. Sharon knew it was one of the most solemn parts of the ceremony, and they were all required to remain silent. His father rubbed the piece of bread three times in a pinch of salt he spread over the table. He took a bite from the salted bread and passed it to his wife and daughter, who did the same.

"Why don't we have any guests tonight?" asked Sharon.

Chaia mumbled an answer but was halted by her husband.

"Tonight is a special night, my dear," he said.

The girl refused to accept that for an answer.

"What is the point of it all?" she said, looking at the wooden cross in the middle of the living room and the crown of thorns on the table beside her.

The man cleared his throat and felt suddenly suffocated.

"It is not for little girls to ask questions to her parents," he said. "Just eat the *gefilte fish* and keep quiet."

Sharon ate some fish by spearing it with her fork and bringing it to her mouth. The metallic tang in her mouth made her gag. She made a mouth gesture as if to speak before falling on the plate.

Chaia, as if nothing had happened, took a piece of the fish in a spoon and took it to her son's mouth. He would not open it, so she had to push it inside and pour the content into his throat. The child fell unconscious almost immediately.

The husband and wife then stood up. He went to the kitchen, opened her blouse, and removed her skirt and underwear. Then she put the crown of thorns on her head. Her husband came back from the kitchen. He was holding a big, rusty meat knife.

They didn't look at one another. They knew what they had to do.

Chaia walked to the wooden cross erected in their living room.

"Where is the bucket?" she asked calmly.

The man went around the house to the back. He returned seconds later, holding a white oak bucket filled with a hammer and iron nails. "It is now time," he said. Chaia laid on the wooden cross. She extended her arms and closed her legs. Her husband gulped. Although he had prepared for that moment for years, he was still nervous.

The man took the hammer and a nail and prayed out loud as fast as he could. Then, he used the hammer to hit the nail into the top of his wife's right hand. He could feel the crack of the bone, her hand tissue coming apart, the muscle being torn apart, and the blood flooding. She didn't say a word or groan. Instead, a single tear came down, swirling from her eyes. After firmly nailing her right hand, he did the same with her left hand. Now, he was praying aloud so he wouldn't hear the iron nail breaking his wife's bones and flesh. He took it to her feet when both hands had been nailed. Even though he only had to do it once, piercing both her feet with a single nail was more painful than piercing her hands and required much more blunt force. Chaia was silent throughout. She shut her eyes and let the tears fall. She was firmly fastened to the cross when the man got up from the floor. He was covered in sweat; he looked at her, crucified on the floor, and then took the chain he'd attached to the ceiling pulley and yanked it with all his remaining strength. The cross took off from the floor. He continued until it was fully erected, carrying her wife's naked, crucified body. Her breathing had increased, and now she was mumbling a prayer. The husband put the white oak bucket on the floor to her left. He counted her ribs with the knife's point from top to bottom and stabbed her between her fourth and fifth ribs. A stream of blood dripped off her chest down to the bucket. He then kissed the knife's spine and, without saying another word, cut off her throat in a single, violent, blasting movement.

She gasped for air for a few seconds, her eyes wide open. Then, her head came down to her chest.

The man then returned to the dinner table, looked at his unconscious daughter and son, and, taking a deep breath, sliced their throats.

He took a chair next to her crucified wife and sat there momentarily, grasping to recover his breath. His hands were all sweaty and trembling. Then, he started praying again, and when the last words of the prayer came out of his mouth, he sliced his own throat. The portrait of the last rebbe of Tikvah Zhytomyr, whose severe glaze emanated from the wall, was his only companion in agonizing moments.

CHAPTER 1

MATT

Matt dug through his pants pockets to find the pack of cigarettes. Then, still naked, he climbed the stairs outside, took the paper, and went back inside. Who still got the news on paper? That was one thing that fascinated him about Laura. There weren't many more, but there was that. She liked old ways, like reading on paper. He knew she probably did that to make herself seem more sophisticated, but he didn't care.

Before sitting down, he put his clothes on, lit a cigarette, and flipped the paper pages. Anything to stay a little longer in Laura's apartment. It was a grey day. The sky was full of big clouds, and little light got into the basement where she lived. Matt was going through the paper pages with little thought when he saw something that caught his eye. His lips trembled, and the cigarette fell to the table. He took it back to his mouth, but his hands also trembled. He felt like his body had transformed into pure anguish.

Laura appeared from the bedroom. She looked like she was still tired; all she had on was her underwear.

"Still here?"

Matt ignored her.

Every Friday night had concluded at her apartment for the past four months. Matt would leave her place as soon as he awoke, and they wouldn't communicate again until the following Friday. Although he had no objection to the tacit understanding, he had been hoping to spend more time with her. He decided not to try it that day but wasn't ready to leave either.

"I am sorry," he stuttered. "I will leave soon."

She walked to the kitchen and filled the electric kettle with water.

"Which do you want?" She showed him two brands of organic coffee and asked him. "Are you a Colombian or an Ethiopian?"

"I don't care," he replied, distracted.

"As you wish," said Laura and went with the Ethiopian. She served two big cups, grabbed one for herself, and offered the other to Matt.

"Are you all right?"

He thought about the best possible answer and found none.

"Yeah, everything is fine. Just having a little slow start today."

They drank the coffee in silence. He looked around, trying to find her eyes, and when he did, she grimaced.

"Okay, time for me to leave."

"You can finish your coffee. Just saying."

"Next Friday?"

"As usual."

He finished his cup of coffee and left her apartment.

As soon as he hit the street, he stopped thinking about Laura and all that silly drama. Now, he felt overtaken by memories of Dave. They had been best friends since childhood and into adolescence until Dave made that life decision nine years ago that Matt could never understand. He was getting to know him again and in the worst way possible. It was not how he would have expected to reunite with that part of his past.

Matt hadn't turned on his phone yet and wasn't willing to do it. Instead, he touched it in the pocket of his pants. That way, he felt he had control over at least one small thing: making himself unavailable to the outside world until he could clarify his ideas. Matt didn't want to hear his mother's cries and desperation or his brother Mike ranting at him.

He walked a few blocks, wanting to get lost in the city and remain anonymous for at least a few hours. Trying to feel confident, he touched his cell phone in his pocket again. It felt as if it weighed a hundred pounds. He walked some more through University Av. until he became tired and boarded the Violet Line in the eastbound direction. He got off at Euston St. station and walked to the one-bedroom apartment that had once belonged to her grandma, *Bubbe* Freida, but was now his to use as much as he pleased. It had been a perfect fit for him since Rashida had ended their seven-year relationship without warning. He climbed the stairs to the second floor and opened the door. There it was, Minerva, at least, to welcome him. The tri-color cat let a single short meow as he entered the apartment. It was her way of welcoming him. Minerva was one of the few things he had been inflexible when negotiating the break-up terms with Rashida. He was the one who discovered the injured cat one night in Garden Park, and it was at his request that they brought her home.

Matt went straight to the TV, turned it on, and, while changing his clothes to more comfortable ones, overheard the news anchor telling the news about the massacre. He changed the channel to hear if anything new was being said. No such luck for him. The little red dot of his old-fashioned answering machine was tilting. Of course, it was. He turned on his computer and read Twitter, where everyone seemed to talk about the same thing. The hashtags #EldersOfZion and #JewishMassacre were trending. He felt disgusted but not surprised.

A torrent of photos of Dave was flushing everywhere: on the TV news, on Twitter, on every news outlet. He knew it was the same Dave Wainstein he had befriended long ago. After reading the Times article, he knew it was him, but he had tried to convince himself otherwise. It couldn't be the same person. But it was. He glanced at Minerva and said, half to her and half to himself, "Can you believe this shit?" The cat yawned at him. "Yeah, me neither," he responded.

The weekend had just started, but he had had it already ruined for him by a deep feeling of unsetting and sadness. Matt took a deep breath and pushed the button on his answering machine.

His mother's screaming voice was the first thing he overheard.

CHAPTER 2

SHAYNA

S he wasn't supposed to be there that night for various reasons. First, it was *Shabbos*, and she had left her house while her parents and brothers were sleeping.

She wasn't used to the dark, the noise, all the people, the food, or the constant touching of bodies. People eating pepperoni pizzas, lobster, bacon, and other forbidden things. She didn't know how those things would taste in her mouth. The temptation to try them was great, but she lacked the will. "Just one transgression at a time," she told herself. Still, she was committing so many sins that night that she was probably wiping out her entire life of strict adherence to the six hundred and thirteen Jewish precepts. At least the ones that can still be followed. "Times change, and so do the precepts," she tried to convince herself. "Isn't it the essence of Jewishness to question certainties all the time?"

She felt like she was about to have a panic attack while sitting at the bar counter.

Above all, she wasn't supposed to be there because she was the daughter of the famous rabbi Moshe Lehrer. But that name meant nothing there. Nobody would be afraid after hearing his name. Nobody would even know who he was. But she did. And when she repeated his name in her head, her body trembled for a second.

"I am already here," she thought, "so I better get used to it."

A well-built bartender came close and asked her,

"What will be for you, princess?"

"*Shabbos* is Queen, and I am a princess. A miscarried princess." She thought.

"Can I have the menu, please?" Shayna answered with a timid voice.

The bartender handed her a sheet of paper with strange cocktail names. She knew nothing about them. It was slightly humiliating. She received a better education than the boys in her community who were sent to the Yeshiva after finishing elementary school and were only taught Jewish law and Torah exegesis. Her education had been liberal in comparison. She had attended an all-girls Jewish school in her community, but she had also worked hard to educate herself on secular topics. Jewish classes bored her. Hearing his father talk at home, she could hear all the same tedious things about the Torah and moral stories from ancient rabbis. Shayna discovered that, in contrast, she was fascinated by secular subjects. Those were the topics that were never brought up in her home or her community. So, she studied the things that most interested her, philosophy and English, alone and hiding from her parents and brothers. By then, her mom had probably discovered her secret habit, but she hadn't told her dad, which Shayna appreciated. For a good reason, Rabbi Moshe Lehrer was the current head of an orthodox Jewish branch that had grown from a handful of poor refugees during World War II to hundreds of thousands of people worldwide.

It would be very damaging to the reputation of the great Rabbi Lehrer if word got out that his daughter had been hiding out in the school library reading Victorian Gothic novels. That was the reason Shayna would not stop doing it. She was drawn to the forbidden, and there were plenty of such things within her reach, given her background.

Getting those books wasn't a simple task. There weren't any in his father's library, which was so packed with religious books that some volumes had to be stacked on the floor. His father considered the books she craved as blasphemous at a minimum when not directly filth and abhorrent.

Shayna's love for the forbidden books began with Mrs. Godwin, her English teacher. Mrs. Godwin had gotten permission from the principal, another rabbi, to teach a shortened version of *Frankenstein* in her classroom. With its captivating, misunderstood monster, that tragic story ignited Shayna's interest in nineteenth-century Gothic literature. She had asked Mrs. Godwin for more recommendations. The old lady was so taken aback by the request that she gave her many more, beginning with the unabridged edition of Mary Shelley's masterpiece. How different it was! And how exciting! All the hidden creation symbology scrapped from the edition Mrs. Godwin had been forced to teach in class was now entirely on display. When Shayna read it for the first time, she felt like a door had been unlocked. She was excited to see what was on the other side.

And she had done it. She had been developing her literary taste, and now she knew the differences between literary genres. She was sure of her tastes. Science fiction was a no-go. She already had the Torah and all the stories his father would tell her about rabbis and Jewish heroes for the fantastic. Although, of course, his father would insist that those tales were recollections of historical facts. The story that Moshe parted the Red Sea with the help of God was not just a bedtime story for kids; it was based on actual events. Naturally, the Jewish people of Prague had been protected by a humanoid creature made of clay known as the Golem. There was no doubt about that! How old were the universe, the sky, and the stars? That was an easy one: 5772 years. No more, no less.

But then, Shayna graduated from high school and immediately lost contact with Mrs. Godwin. She had now to take care of her little brothers and prepare to marry soon, with someone she didn't even know. She knew her father had been talking to a local *shadchan*, a matchmaker, who would present him with several eligible young men to choose her spouse. But Shayna didn't want that. She didn't want to settle down with another boring, religious man who would tell her she couldn't keep reading her favorite Gothic books and tell her she had to stay home and have kids for as long as her body could make babies.

She was there because she wanted to see the outside world and wouldn't sit still and let other men decide what to do with her life. Not her father, not her future husband. She'd chosen that bar for her transgression because it was only a short walk from her father's house, where his family slept soundly, unconcerned about her whereabouts. She didn't need the transit to get there. It was forbidden to drive or even be in a car on the *Shabbos*, and she didn't want to break yet another rule if she didn't have to.

Shayna had ordered nothing at the bar yet. She counted how much money she was carrying. It wasn't much. When her family had gone to bed after celebrating the *Kabbalas Shabbos*, she had seen a window of opportunity and seized it without second thoughts. She had sneaked out of her bedroom, trying not to attract attention. It had been a simple task, as everybody had been depleted of energy following the long festivity. Although Shayna was tired, the excitement of what she was doing kept her awake. Aside from caring for her brothers, she had helped her mother cook that night, trying to beat the clock so the stove burners wouldn't still be on at seven when the first star rose in the sky. Then, they did their best to keep the food warm until about ten, when the great Rabbi Lehrer returned from the synagogue with guests. They would never know how many guests he would bring, so they always cooked in excess, just in case, so that nobody was left without a warm serving of *gefilte fish*.

A man was sitting next to her with a glass of whisky. He seemed lost in his thoughts as he looked at the bottles of liquor lined up behind the bar counter.

"Hi, I'm sorry," she told him. "Could you suggest something to drink from this list?"

The man was caught off guard. He grabbed the menu and took a quick look.

"I'm not sure if you're allowed to drink anything other than soda. So, if I were you, I'd pick a Diet Coke," he told Shayna.

She blushed as she felt the blood flowing through her veins directly into her face.

"Hey Mark, have you asked this young lady for her ID yet?" the man asked the bartender.

"I am twenty-one," she said.

"I don't want any trouble," said the bartender.

"Then present your ID to him. I respect Mark and the business he runs here," said the man. "I don't want it closed down just because he sold alcohol to a minor. And you don't look like you're twenty-one at all."

Shayna was now furious. Of course, she was of legal age. And she had been drinking vodka since she was eighteen. The best part of Kabbalas Shabbos was when dinner was over, and vodka was passed around until everyone was so drunk they had to go to sleep so they wouldn't fall on the floor.

"Your ID, please," said Mark.

She didn't have one with her. She hadn't considered that before leaving her father's house.

"I left it at my place," she said, trying to sound confident.

"Well, then I will need to ask you to leave the premises," said Mark, taking the menu from her hand. She felt his fingers touching her, and she felt repulsion. She wasn't supposed to touch any adult man except her future husband, only after they married. Even his father was off limits since she had her first period. And now, her fingers and skin had touched those of another filthy man.

She had thought that going to the outside world wouldn't be so hard or different. She had been wrong. Shayna felt terrible about touching another man's skin more than anything she knew she'd done wrong that night. She felt humiliated.

"What's wrong with you?" asked the bartender.

"You touched me."

"So?"

"Aren't you afraid that I might be impure?"

"Impure? What are you talking about?"

"You know... that I may be having my period right now. Blood makes women impure." Shayna explained without thinking as if she was pointing out the obvious. Almost immediately, she regretted saying that. She wasn't supposed to teach every non-Jew she met along the way.

After looking at each other, the two men laughed.

"Are you one of those crazy Jewish people who live next door?" asked the man she had asked for advice on what to drink.

The bartender poured a glass of something transparent and gave it to her.

"It is late, and almost nobody is here. Take one from the house."

"Are... are you sure?" Shayna asked.

"Please don't tell anyone. And don't come back unless you bring an ID."

She took the glass and drank it in one large sip.

"That was pure vodka," she said and coughed.

"Didn't you say you are used to drinking it?" the bartender asked.

"Yes."

"Now get the fuck out of here."

She walked out of the bar. The two men were now talking and laughing, and she couldn't help but feel like they were laughing at her. She was pathetic. Everything that she had done was wrong. Even drinking that glass of vodka. She hadn't said the *SheHaKol* blessing before drinking it because she feared being mocked by those two horrendous men. Everything had been awful, and she was now feeling guilty about it all. And for what? just to waste time in a bar chatting with a pair of jerks. So that people would make fun of her for being Jewish and a woman.

She could think of many reasons she shouldn't have been there that night. But the main reason she shouldn't have gone there in the first place was something she couldn't know then. And that reason was that at that very second, her sister was being crucified not too far away, and her brother-in-law was slitting the throats of her nephews.

CHAPTER 3

MATT

He listened to his mother's phone messages until about the middle of the fifth, when he got bored. With each new message, starting with "Dear son, have you seen the news today?" her tone of desperation became clearer. Finally, the last one he heard said, "Call me right away!"

It was almost ten years since he and David had grown apart, and they had had no contact for the last six years.

Matt pushed the stop button from the answering machine and sat in the bed's frame. He felt like he couldn't stop feeling dizzy. It was as if someone had kicked him in the head and knocked him down, and he had just gotten up again. Minerva cuddled against his feet. He hoped to sleep until Monday to return to his freelance content writing gig and forget what had happened. Matt suddenly remembered that he had agreed to meet Josh and one of his friends that night to go out for drinks. Josh had insisted that he met that friend of his, but Matt had always found an excuse. In the end, Matt still wanted things to get serious with Laura, so he didn't feel the need to meet any other girls for the moment. He realized he would need to cancel that night's plan, as he wouldn't want to talk with Josh or his friend about David. Matt was sure that the matter would be mentioned. He knew people would talk about what had happened. More considering it had happened there, in the Big City. The city was stuffed with its daily craziness, but not with this kind of horror. There was also the issue of Jewish people being involved. Orthodox Jews to make things worse.

"*Payot*," he recalled David telling him many years back when he laughed at the sidelocks his friend had grown out of nowhere.

"And why are you wearing them?"

"You wouldn't understand."

That was true. He had never understood why his friend suddenly started acting so weird. They both came from Jewish families. Assimilated Jewish families in which religion was non-existent, Hebrew was a foreign language, Yiddish was the language their *bubbes* spoke with their immigrant parents, and Jewish holidays were simply an excuse for the family to get together without regard for tradition. And then, one day, with no previous sign, David had grown *payot* and started eating kosher only, wearing black robes and a *shtreimel*.

The sharp sound of the doorbell brought him back to the present day. He stepped onto the balcony and noticed his brother standing in the street, waiting for him to open the door while on the phone. Although it was Saturday noon, he wore a white shirt, a black blazer, and a tie as if about to go to the office.

Matt opened the door for his brother, who was still on the phone. He walked in.

"Ok, welcome, I guess," Matt muttered.

Mike entered the apartment and continued talking by phone for a few minutes. After that, Matt retrieved two glasses of water from the fridge and offered one to him.

"About time you showed your face!" his brother exclaimed when he hung up.

"Nice to see you, too."

"Why the fuck didn't you call Mom back? She has been calling you all morning! Have you seen the news yet?"

"Yeah,"

"Are you going to keep hiding?"

"Calm down. It has been a tough day."

"You bet it has! I am in the middle of a big corporation merger and had to deal with Mom worrying about your sorry ass all morning!"

"You're always in the middle of something big. A big corporation merger, a big case, a big whatever."

"A big cock up your ass is what you will get if you don't get your shit together."

"Fuck off. If you came here to bitch me around, you could just fuck off."

"Calm down, little brother. By the way, can you offer me some coffee? But please, for the love of God, don't give me that microwave-warmed instant coffee crap you have from three days ago, like the last time."

"I am sorry I am not in the position to buy a fancy espresso machine, but I will provide you with a fresh instant coffee cup if you take it."

"I think I'll have to, don't I? Or, better yet, why don't we go to *The Orchid* for an early dinner?"

Matt would never agree to eat with his brother on that day.

"I don't like sushi. I thought you would know by now."

"Whatever. Do you prefer *El Inka*? How about some ceviche?"

"That also has uncooked fish in it."

"I understand why you can't get a girl to stay with you."

Rather than respond, Matt went to prepare the instant coffee. They stayed silent for a moment. After hearing his brother almost scream and spit all those words, Matt felt like he was recovering from a terrible hangover. When the coffee was ready, he poured it into a mug and brought it to Mike.

"This is going to give me an ulcer," he said after a short sip.

"It is what it is."

"A piece of shit. That is what it is. It is literally like drinking diarrhea. I can give you my old Nespresso. I got a new one."

Of course, he did. Mike couldn't resist bragging about his success.

"I wouldn't want it. Those capsules are expensive. And an ecologic hazard."

"I will provide you with those damn capsules," said Mike, "at least so that you can offer me something drinkable next time I pay you a visit."

"Anything else?"

"Yes, indeed. Are we finished pretending we don't see the elephant in the room?"

"I know nothing about this," said Matt. "I haven't seen David in years. So I am as surprised as you, Mom, or anyone else."

"I don't give a damn about that lunatic. It is you I am concerned about."

Matt looked at his brother.

"Because Mom is worried, of course."

There, there it was. So he had to level down his affection for him.

"I'm not sure what to think. I am surprised, of course."

"And?"

"And what?"

"Anything else?"

"Well, yes. I mean. I feel indifference. David was my best friend for many years. As we grew apart and he embraced this whole Orthodox Jewish thing, it's almost as if the person who did all these horrible things in the news today was a completely different person than the one I used to know."

Mike walked around the place.

"You have a lot of useless shit in this tiny apartment," he said, pointing to a stack of books on the floor.

"Thank you. That is for a project I am working on."

"You surely stretch the meaning of 'project,' don't you?"

Mike kept strolling around the apartment as if inspecting it. Then he approached Matt and, grabbing his shoulders, said, "Look, little brother, you can spend as much time as you want in this shithole. All I want you to do is call Mom and reassure her that everything is fine and will be fine in the future. Please don't speak to her as you did to me; she'll freak out that you're 'indifferent' about your suicidal baby-killer friend. You know how she gets. She is getting old, and we must try to make her life easier since she lost Dad."

He was right about this. It was the only thing Mike had said that day that made sense.

"Apart from this, how are you doing?"

"Fine, everything is fine."

He knew Mike wasn't asking because he cared but because it was what he was supposed to do. In the end, what he answered was irrelevant. He could just say, "My life is a fucking disaster," and get the same tap on his shoulder from Mike.

"Just fine? Any girl crazy enough to one day become my sister-in-law, maybe?"

"I don't think so."

"No? And what happened to that Rashida you have been seeing?"

"We broke up almost a year ago."

"A year? And how's it I knew nothing about this?"

"You ask that yourself. I told you when it happened."

"I thought it was just a short-term thing, and you'd be back to normal soon like you have been many times before."

"Well, no. This time, it was definitive."

"I see."

Matt knew that deep inside, Mike was relieved. He had never liked Rashida. Matt had always wondered if it had had something to do with her skin color. He preferred not to think about that.

"Sometimes I can't believe that we are related. You never tell me anything about the girls you are banging!"

"There is always someone. Don't worry about me."

"And living in this crappy place. Writing shitty pieces for shitty websites. I don't get you."

"This was *Bubbe's* house. If you don't remember."

"Yeah, I know."

"Anyway, what about you? Are you still cheating on your wife with that chick you met at the gym?"

Mike didn't expect that jab from his silly brother.

"You bastard, don't you dare to talk to me like that!"

"Look, I don't care where you put your dick in. I feel a little sorry about Karen, of course. She is a nice woman and doesn't deserve you fucking around. But it is your thing, your decision, your life. Just try not to hurt the girls."

"I think I've had enough of this," said Mike, preparing to leave.

"Great. I never invited you, by the way."

Mike got so close that he could feel him breathe.

"If I came here, it was because you couldn't answer the phone for Mom, you smartass. In case you don't recall, she is an old woman alone in this world, except for you and me. She worries that one of his son's best friends has become a maniac killer. Apart from that, you can do whatever you like with your excuse for a life. Keep living in this shithole, keep scaring any woman stupid enough to show some interest in you, and do as you please, but you don't get to mess with Mom. Or me and my family. Did I make myself clear?"

The two brothers looked at each other for a few seconds.

"I am leaving now," said Mike, giving up and leaving the apartment.

"Checkmate," thought Matt as he prepared to call his mom and tell her everything was fine.

CHAPTER 4

SHAYNA

I t was as if she'd hit her head a thousand times. She felt completely ridiculous. After Shabbos' dinner, her dad and uncles would drink heavily, but she had never seen them feel so awful the next day. Worst of all, she still had to linger through the rest of the day and its promise of boring contemplation of life.

Unlike the rest of her family, Shayna believed that the rules that came with the first star on Friday and were removed with the first star on Saturday were a source of stress rather than happiness and freedom. There were so many prohibitions to observe that almost nothing was left to do. It was supposed to be a time when she could focus on herself, draw closer to God, and relieve stress. However, that required rest was surrounded by so many rules and bans on "getting involved with the world" that she didn't have time to do the things that would help her relax. What about going out for lunch? Impossible. You weren't allowed to touch money. And, of course, she was dying to go out to one of those fancy restaurants that she was always forbidden to enter as they didn't serve kasher. What about going to a park and lying in the grass as the sun warmed her face? Not in this life. What about hanging out with friends? Not during *Shabbos*. How could she relax if she couldn't even use the subway that day? She wasn't even allowed to pick up the keys to her house because it was considered a struggle. Instead, she was supposed to spend the entire afternoon meditating, praying, and finding joy in those things. On some rare occasions, her father would allow her to go for a short walk around High Park on Saturday afternoons. Still, she always had to be accompanied by her mother. For Shayna, those walks were almost worse than staying at home. They would walk in silence, and Shayna would think about all the things she didn't dare say to her father's face. She would also feel jealous of the people in the park who could live as they wished.

Meanwhile, her father would study silently with her siblings behind his studio's closed doors. He never grew tired of that routine. It was almost as if studying the Torah and the

Talmud held him. Without that, he would be lost in the world. And maybe that was the reason he was so strict. But Shayna knew underneath his father's easygoing demeanor was a straightforward, sometimes cruel man.

At least that day, she didn't feel like going out. Last night had been too intense, and she still felt the adrenaline riding through her veins. She had taken too many risks. She couldn't imagine what her father would do if he found out about her Friday night. Shayna knew what he had done to her sister when he found out she didn't follow the rules about keeping *Shabbos*. Shayna could never forgive her father for what he had done to Chaia. She had kept her feelings for herself, growing angry and hateful toward him for what he had done to her sister. Behind the good rabbi his community saw was an angry man who would let no one question his decisions. She was certain he would at least listen or discuss with her if she were a man. But she was just a woman and had to conform and keep quiet.

Although she knew how things had ended, Shayna didn't know exactly what Chaia had done that precipitated her father's bold decision. It had all passed eight years ago when Shayna was nine and her older sister twenty. Their age difference of eleven years coincided with the time the rabbi and her mother couldn't conceive. They did as the Torah mandates in the *Bereishit*: "Be fertile and increase, fill the earth." The rabbi had met his duties as a husband, but until Shayna came along, they couldn't conceive any more children. After her, almost every other year, a new child was born: Yair, Joel, Joseph, and Mendel. And then it stopped again. Six children seemed oddly low for a Tikvahh Zhytomyr family, but it was much worse coming from the community's leader. He was supposed to have at least ten, possibly up to fifteen or seventeen, but because he was the leader of his community, most people refrained from criticizing him and his wife. Not that people didn't talk about it behind their backs, but it wasn't openly discussed.

The same thing went for Chaia. Nobody in the community would talk about her after her father had expelled her from his house and the community. Shayna remembered that day when she heard her sister's and father's last discussion. She remembered the rabbi's studio door being violently closed, enclosing Chaia and her father, and then how the discussion began and quickly devolved into an uproar of shouts and her sister crying loudly. She admired how Chaia had the temple to confront his father, although, at that moment, she didn't get what their discussion was about. Shayna thought she could not defy the rabbi, yet her sister had done it and had paid the price. When the rabbi spoke at home, the women would listen and follow his instructions.

When Chaia and her father talked that afternoon, they talked for hours. It had almost turned into a rabbinical debate, another reason his father had become so enraged with her. How could his own daughter defy him in rabbinical terms? Shayna had tried to enter the room and stop them from screaming, but her mother had forbidden her to intervene. Instead, she had stayed hidden behind his father's studio door, intent on eavesdropping their conversation. There had been moments of silence, which gave Shayna hope they had reconciled. Still, after just a few minutes or even hours of tense silence, the shouts started again.

And then, there was a long, long silence. It was so pronounced that Shayna feared her sister and her father would die inside the studio. Maybe they had killed themselves, or each other, or both had heart attacks due to so much shouting and discussion. After one hour of that silence, Shayna entered the studio and checked if they were still alive. At that exact moment, her sister came out without looking back. She went all the way down the hallway to the door without even noticing Shayna's presence and then stormed out of the house, closing the door furiously. Chaia would never cross that door again. That had been the penultimate time Shayna would see her. The last time had been by pure chance when she saw her in the street. Chaia was pushing a stroller with two babies while walking with a man. It was almost the start of *Shabbos,* and they were calmly walking. She hadn't dared to approach them. Apart from that encounter, out of pure chance, she hadn't seen her sister or heard anything from her.

Following the discussion and her sister's abrupt departure, Shayna entered her father's studio and saw him as she had never seen him before: the man was sitting behind his desk, surrounded by old dusty books, some of which were open; he was touching his eyes, had the head inclined forward, and his long white beard was full of little saliva particles that had fallen there when shouting and discussing. But what most affected Shayna that day was seeing two transparent tears falling down his cheeks. The rabbi was crying.

That night, as the family sat at the table, the air seemed too thick to breathe, and there was total silence, broken only by the sound of the forks hitting the plates. Chaia's name was never spoken aloud again, and Shayna never had the nerve to ask why.

All those memories returned to haunt Shayna that dull *Shabbos* afternoon while she still felt her head vibrating with every sound surrounding her. And then the telephone in the house started ringing. Someone had forgotten to disconnect the line before the mandatory rest day began. It was a severe offense in the eyes of the rabbi, as it would disrupt the silence and tranquility required by such a sacred day.

Shayna's hangover amplified the ring's loud, penetrating sound. She knew it would be another ten rings before the answering machines rolled. The phone rang until his father's recorded voice asked the caller to leave a message in Yiddish, Hebrew, and English. She knew the rabbi would talk to the family that night about how someone had forgotten to turn off the phone before *Shabbos*. Everyone had to follow the rules, and everyone had a role assigned. He wouldn't refer directly to the person responsible for that error. Everyone knew, however, that the women of the house had to take care of the preparations for *Shabbos* to enjoy it as the Mosaic law required.

After the first caller hung up, the telephone rang again. The rabbi sighed, marking his discomfort as he accommodated in his desk chair, not taking his sight away from the book he was reading. Shayna was also reading a book while sitting on a couch outside the rabbi's office. She liked to sit there where she could glance at him occasionally when his studio door was open. Despite all the differences between them and all the things she didn't like about the man, she still admired and loved him as much as he loved her.

When the phone rang for the third time, the rabbi carefully put down the book he was reading, removed his bulky glasses, closed his eyes, took a deep breath, moved his arms to help the blood flow again, and politely asked:

"Dear daughter, do you know why the telephone line was not turned off before the beginning of *Shabbos*?"

Shayna had passed the last hour remembering her sister and feeling her head crunching. Then, the rabbi's words jolted her back to the present.

"I am sorry. I was distracted. What was that you were asking me?"

"It is a simple question. Do you know why the telephone is ringing during *Shabbos*?"

"I don't know. It must have passed someone."

"That seems pretty obvious," the rabbi remarked ironically.

"I am so sorry. I will make sure that this doesn't happen again."

The rabbi clicked his tongue, removed his glasses, and returned to reading the enormous book before him. Then, the telephone started ringing again. This time, the caller left a message. He told the rabbi he was a journalist and wanted to discuss the massacre. He sent condolences almost automatically, then asked if that was a Jewish custom.

Although Shayna did not know what the journalist was talking about, she was intrigued by the message.

"Maybe we should answer the next time," she told her father.

"And maybe you should shut up and stop saying silly things," the rabbi answered.

The phone rang again, but the caller didn't leave a message this time. After him, a steady stream of calls came in. Some callers were now leaving more and more messages, asking for the rabbi to call back and offering brief, embarrassing condolences.

Shayna went to look for her mother, who was reading Hasidic tales to her brothers. The phone was ringing once again.

"Mother, I am a little worried about all these calls we are receiving. Maybe we should answer the phone."

Without looking up from the book she was reading, the woman said, "That is forbidden, as you know." The rabbi then appeared and ordered Shayna to disconnect the line for good.

"This issue is causing so much frustration that it is ruining *Shabbos*. Therefore, disconnecting the line is preferable," he said.

Shayna assented but immediately tried again to change his father's opinion.

"It seems important. Why don't we pick up the phone the next time?"

"Absolutely no. Impossible," the rabbi said with impatience.

Shayna was about to disconnect the phone line when the doorbell rang. It rang a few more times. Shayna looked at his father, who appeared worried. Finally, he got up from his desk.

"Enough!" he exclaimed. "I'm on my way to the temple. Today, it is impossible to adhere to the obligations in this house." He sounded bitter.

The rabbi grabbed his coat, put on his hat, carried a pack of books under his arm, and left the house. At the gates, there was a group of people mounting a guard that went to surround him. Cameras and microphones suddenly appeared around his head. They asked him about her dead daughter, how he had received the news, what he planned to do, and if there would be an official statement from Tikvah Zhytomyr.

The rabbi found himself completely overwhelmed, incapable of grasping what was happening.

"My daughter is alive and well inside the house. What are you referring to?"

"Your other daughter," someone said.

"Chaia Wainstein!" shouted a journalist holding a microphone just before his face.

All the television cameras focused on him, expecting his first words to acknowledge what had happened.

A now tired man looking like he had put twenty years in just seconds angrily shouted, "I don't have and never had a daughter named Chaia!" He pushed his way back inside the house.

CHAPTER 5

MATT

Matt noticed Laura's breast gently rising and falling. This was the first time she had spent the night at his place. Also, it was Thursday, not Friday. They had broken two of the rules she had established as soon as they started seeing each other: that they would only date on Friday nights and that they would only go to her place.

He liked her, even though he knew she was a snob, a cynic, and a little bitchy.

The moonlight poured from the balcony. It was 3.24 a.m., and Matt hadn't been able to sleep for an hour, according to the cheap digital clock on his desk. He got up and searched for a small metal box hidden under his underwear and socks in the drawer. He found a joint, took it, and went to the balcony to smoke it. The streets outside were empty except for the occasional addict screaming to the moon. He was so used to those people that it was as if they weren't there. He enjoyed being alone on the balcony, smoking, and not thinking about anything.

An icy hand touched his back. It was Laura. She was undressed and waved her hand for him to pass the joint.

"Can't sleep, big boy?"

"So it seems."

"Yeah, me neither."

They both remained silent for a moment.

"Let's go back to bed," she told him.

He returned inside, but he didn't immediately go to sleep. Instead, he sat down in front of his computer and began typing.

"Aren't you coming?" asked Laura, who was lying down and waiting for him.

"In a minute," he said.

He attempted to condense some thoughts for an upcoming news piece about the e-book industry that BuzzFeed had commissioned him to write. Still, he couldn't come up with anything meaningful. He typed a few words, read them, and then deleted them, frustrated. He then went back to sleep. It wasn't long before he nodded off. He was awakened in the morning by the sunlight touching his face. Laura had already left.

Just as Matt was about to get up, the phone rang.

"Hello?" said tiredly.

"Matthew. Do you still recall me?" a solemn female voice on the other end of the line said.

Yes, he recognized that voice. That smoking, deep and imposing voice.

"It's Margaret," said the voice before he could answer. "Margaret Wainstein" added as if it was necessary.

"Yeah, I know. How are you, Margaret? It has been a long time."

"Cut it. We don't need this now. I want to talk to you in person."

"Well, I don't know. But, I mean, yeah, I am sorry I didn't call you before regarding David, of course."

"I don't need this from you, my dear Matthew. However, I would appreciate it if you could meet me. I won't take much of your time."

Matt cursed in silence.

"I am swamped for the next weeks and can't tell when I'll have some free time."

"Oh, you are coming right now," the woman said firmly. "A man is waiting for you downstairs from your apartment. His name is Carlos Ortega. He will bring you to my office."

"But I have just come out of bed!" Matt tried to argue.

"So what? Get dressed, wash your face, and leave."

Matt bit his lower lip. He knew there was no point in contradicting Margaret Wainstein. In the meantime, Minerva had also woken up and was staring at him, passively letting him know she was expecting him to feed her.

"I'll be there. Just tell your driver to wait for me to get dressed and feed my cat."

He heard the *click* on the other side of the line. Margaret Wainstein didn't enjoy wasting a single second. He put some clothes in, filled Minerva's food pot, and splashed water into his face. He went down the stairs to the street. Waiting for him in front of a black Mercedes Benz was a Mexican man of about sixty, a little overweight, wearing sunglasses, and sporting a full mustache.

"Matthew, I assume?" said the man.

They shook hands.

"Carlos Ortega, I assume."

"You assume right," said the man while opening the back door for Matt.

He got on board.

"What happened to Willy?" asked Matt.

"He retired a few years ago," the driver responded, entering the cabin. "I've been working for Mrs. Wainstein since."

"I see." Matt felt like he had nothing else to talk about.

The trip to Margaret Wainstein's office downtown seemed surreal to him. The sky was heavy with grey clouds that announced an imminent rain.

"Do you know why Mrs. Wainstein wants to see me?" he asked the driver.

"You ask her, kid," said the man condescendingly.

"Of course, it is just that with Willy, we kind of had this relationship of confidence, and I thought that maybe..."

"Anything Mrs. Wainstein has to say to you will say it herself."

A tense silence followed.

"You don't seem to have been a driver all your life. I am wrong?"

"Back in my time, I was with the police. In my home country, why ask?"

"No particular reason," said Matt, and he knew that was the hint to shut up.

They finally arrived at a tall, bland building near Stanley Park. The driver entered the private underground parking and drove to the reserved spot.

"Follow me," he said as they exited the car and entered an internal elevator. He entered a code in the buttons panel, and the elevator took them off to a private suite on the forty-fifth floor. When the lift doors opened, they were welcomed by a marvelous spectacle of white marble walls and bright floors. At the end of what seemed like an endless hall, Margaret Wainstein was sitting behind a large oak desk. She was surrounded by fine furnishings, including two plush all-leather Chesterfield sofas, a coffee table piled high with bottles of the finest scotch whisky, and a wall of bookshelves that reached from floor to ceiling.

Guzmán gestured for Matt to sit in a red velvet chair.

He took the seat, feeling slightly uncomfortable.

"Hello," he said timidly.

The woman answered by throwing him a file folder filled with photos.

"Look," she said while keeping her sight on a document she held with her other hand.

Matt did as instructed and took the photos. He immediately felt ill. There were pictures of David and his family's crime scene. She may have gotten them straight from the police, as they had never been published. The sight was truly disgusting. Detailed shots of the kid's slashed throats, RX of broken bones where the nails have been pushed through, David's final resting face, and a panoramic view of the crime scene.

"So? What do you think?" said Margaret Wainstein.

"Why are you showing me these?"

"My only son is dead, and you are complaining?"

"I'm sorry, but I don't understand why you're showing me the photos."

"You know I wasn't even allowed to take part in his burial? They took care of everything. As always."

"Who's they?"

"They! Those retarded bastards that wear black all day and night no matter the humidity and the heat in this sweltering city!"

"I... I don't know what to say."

"Then shut up and listen to me," said the woman, reclining in her chair. "You know I don't blame you for what happened. But let's be honest, David was never the same after the accident."

Matt knew that was coming. For her purported not blaming game, it was pretty damning.

"He started seeing those maniacs when he was recovering in the hospital. The medics had told me he had little chance of survival. I think those monsters came for me. They flew around him like crows when they found I would not engage in their shenanigans and that David was not dead but recovering."

"I know he didn't want to go to that party. I was the one who insisted he came along with me," said Matt.

"You knew he'd always had feelings for Rashida. And you didn't seem to mind. Instead, you insisted on him accompanying you. On the day she introduced you to her friends and family as her boyfriend. How could you possibly be so cold?"

"I... I don't know. We were young, and he was my best friend. I had no intention of hurting him."

"And then you had to get drunk and insist that you were perfectly fine to drive back from the party."

"I made many mistakes in my life and on that night," admitted Matt, "but I am not responsible for what happened with him after that."

"Of course, you aren't. And yet, you survived the accident without a single scratch. My poor Dave had to spend a month in the hospital. And it was then, when he was the most vulnerable, that those Hasidim from hell preyed upon him. Every time I think about them, those dirty, long beards, those awful *payot* coming from the sides of their awful heads, those cords coming from their hips, they are just awful, awful people."

Matt said nothing. He knew she was exaggerating because of her pain.

"Not even my grandfather, a brutish Polish peasant, would wear those hideous black robes in the summer," said the woman, finally letting go of some of her anger.

"He almost died, Matt," she continued. "The doctors told me he had brain damage and would never be the same, even if he survived. Those people took advantage of that. They were around his bed, making him pray. He had never prayed before! He hadn't even had a *bar mitzvah*! They transformed him. And now see where he ended."

Matt felt there was a deeper reason for him being there than for Margaret Wainstein to unload all her anger over her son's demise.

"The case is being closed," she said at last. "According to the police, this was a murder-suicide. They claim there is not much more to look into."

"I am sorry to hear that."

"My son and his insane wife. I'd never met her. Or the kids, my grandchildren. He would forbid me to approach them if I did not agree to conform to their beliefs. I made it clear to him I would never, ever accommodate to the half-cooked customs of those misogynist fuckers of Tikvah Zhytomyr." She sighed, "Ortega, bring me my checks."

The man reappeared out of nowhere, carrying a checkbook.

Margaret Wainstein took it from his hands and, pointing a pen to it, said,

"Let's cut to the chase. How much do you want to work for me?"

"What?"

"Is ten thousand enough? I can give you five thousand and the rest when you finish what I will ask you to do."

Matt hadn't expected that at all. He had thought about a million reasons Margaret Wainstein may have brought him there, including the recriminations she had poured over him. Still, he never thought she would offer money to do anything.

"I must admit that I am a little surprised."

"Fifteen thousand then?"

"It... it is not about the money."

"Eighteen thousand. Last offer. Take it or leave it."

"Please, I want to know what you want me to do for you!"

"I need you to infiltrate them. Those Hasidim. Tikvah Zhytomyr."

"What?!"

"Am I not clear enough? What do you think, Carlos?"

"I think you are being clear, madam."

"Exactly. It is straightforward. I need you to start the path my son took. I want you to attend their meetings, engage with them, and dress like them. You need to tell me why my son did what he did."

"Don't you have a better-suited candidate than me for this job?"

"What better candidate than you? As my son, you are a secular Jew. You are still young and single. You are the perfect prey for them."

Matt felt uncomfortable. That description was on point, which made it so distressing.

Margaret Wainstein wrote eight thousand dollars in a check and handed it to Matt.

"I am not sure this is right for me to do. Accepting this money would feel like betraying Dave."

"I think you've already betrayed him enough. Now accept the money and get to work."

It was certainly an amount that would give him peace of mind for the following months, but it didn't feel like something he was willing to do.

"If I cash this check, where should I look first?"

"You are an intelligent young man, Matthew. Besides, they are everywhere. Have you been to Citadel Square on a Friday at six in the afternoon? There they are, trying to convince every Jew-looking male to put *tefillin*."

He was still not convinced.

"This is something you must do, Matthew. Do it not for me but for David. Do it for all the other kids who have been co-opted into this sect. We must act now before these brainwashers destroy more families."

Even though Matt thought he had to be a fool not to take such easy money, he was still unconvinced.

Chapter 6

Shayna

Shayna wasn't paying attention to what the man was saying, but she knew what he was saying. After all, it couldn't be so different from anything other men like him could tell her. She was feeling tired of hearing those things repeatedly. Still, the man in front of her was a young rabbinical promise. After hearing the first two minutes of his undisturbed, monotonous monologue, Shayna switched off her brain and stopped listening.

His hat was on the table near him, a simple black yarmulke covered his balding head, and his black jacket hung from his chair. Aside from that, he wore a cream-colored waistcoat over a white shirt and a black velvet tie with white spots. The waistcoat and shirt were so close to his body that it almost looked like they were a second skin.

Shayna didn't have to be at that dinner to figure out every tedious detail. The man she had in front of her, who hadn't stopped talking to her for a second, had been born and lived in Queen Elevation until he was eighteen when he was sent to Tikvah Zhytomyr's Yeshiva in Jerusalem. There, he had spent the last five years studying and perfecting his Kabbalah knowledge. He was rumored to be a prodigy, unmatched by his classmates. His teachers, seasoned rabbis, would sit down with him for hours to debate the finer points as if he were one of them. And now he was back in the city and having dinner with Shayna. Their wedding was already planned, but they had to go on a date before it could happen. For someone who had never been on one before, Shayna found the experience to be rather tedious. No physical contact was permitted, including holding hands; they could only eat together and converse. Even then, it had to be done surrounded by other Hasidim. Their fathers set up the wedding, and that they were distant cousins hadn't been a problem. To ensure a good match, their DNA was compared. Since they were there, Shayna assumed that everything had gone well. That meant it was unlikely that she and Mordechai Posner would have children who inherited degenerative diseases from their community's inbreeding. "We're a big family living in tents; forty percent of Ashkenazim are descendants of four women," Shayna thought, "the remaining sixty percent come from just one hundred and fifty women." She had read about that in a book forbidden in the community that she had found in the public library. "We are all related in the end. No wonder we have an increased risk of developing Tay-Sachs or other nasty diseases. But it will be fine. It has to be fine. Our tests must have shown that our future children's chances of developing those illnesses are slim." She kept thinking, superimposing her internal voice to the one of Mordechai Posner. That man was still talking to her. She was not impressed by his prestige and credentials but was more interested in looking at how his long beard was shaped like a maze. Shayna couldn't find anything interesting about him. Everything he was saying was boring, and he looked like any other guy in the Tikvah community.

"Zionists are the true evil," said Mordechai Posner. "They are the enemy of the people of Israel."

What was he expecting to provoke in Shayna with that assertion? Not that she hadn't heard that a million times before. Maybe he was trying to show her he was a genuinely pious man, a genuine believer, and a true Hasid.

"I can assure you, right now, that when the time comes, and we move to Mea Shearim in Jerusalem, we will not serve the Zionists. Our children will never bear the genocidal uniforms of the IDF."

He was talking about the Israel Defense Forces or IDF, Israel's army. She knew what he was talking about but didn't think it was appropriate for a first date. It was like listening to a boring, bland reading of the periodic table of the elements.

Shayna was momentarily confused before realizing that Mordechai Posner awaited her response. "I completely agree with you," she said. A slight smile formed on Mordechai Posner's face, but he said nothing.

There was still plenty of food on the table that she hadn't eaten. On another occasion, she wouldn't leave *kneidlach* soup or pastrami. Still, she felt even less appetite than the desire to be there.

"*Az me ken nit vi me vil, muz men vellen vi me ken,*" thought Shayna. "If you can't do what you like, like what you can do," repeated her head in English. She knew what she had to do.

"Excuse me for a second," said Shayna and walked to the washroom.

She momentarily stopped under the door frame and prayed, thanking God for giving her the body orifices she needed to live a healthy life. She was whispering the words when she felt something was off. Shayna felt she was acting like a robot. She didn't even need to go to the washroom. It was just an excuse to get off the table and Mordechai Posner. She walked in and went right to the mirror to look at herself. The reflection was of a woman; she had converted into a woman and hadn't even realized it until that moment. It may have happened because of the pain after her sister's death. As if Chaia's tragedy wasn't enough, her father had brought her additional pain by forbidding any mention of her sister's name or allowing the family to engage in the funeral rites. Nobody in her family had brought their clothing to rags; the mirrors in the house had remained uncovered, and no *kaddish* prayer had been elevated for Chaia. Life had just gone on as if nothing had happened. The news about the crime had been suppressed inside Tikvah Zhytomyr's community, and no one dared to talk about that, at least not in public. His father had continued his duties as usual. A close group of rabbis had joined forces to keep insidious journalists as far as possible from disturbing him and his family. Chaia was never to be mentioned again. The worst part was that only his father was aware of the causes.

She opened the faucet, let some water flow to wet her hands and face, and then went out of the washroom. She avoided the table where her fiance was waiting and slipped out of the restaurant without him noticing.

"If you can't do what you like, like what you can do," repeated Shayna as she reached the outside.

CHAPTER 7

MATT

He stayed in his apartment for the next week, leaving only to buy food and take short walks in Glen Park.

The check Margaret Wainstein gave him had been on his desk since he returned from their meeting. He hadn't agreed to work for her yet, but he couldn't come with the strength to tear it up and flush it down the toilet, even more so when he was making ends meet by penning terrible, pointless articles for websites that paid him little.

Like other times when he had felt life had gotten the better of him, he had found safety in solitude. He had turned off his cell phone and had only picked up landline calls from his mother and once his brother after hearing them leaving a message on the answering machine. His mother was still worried about him and had asked to rejoin the "world of the living people," as she had put it. His brother had said the same, but more impatiently and violently. Matt knew he had only called him because their mother had made him.

While Mike had always been closer than him to their mother, Matt knew he was her favorite since at least the death of their father. It had been three years since the day Big Richard's heart failed. Mike had taken to him to look after their newly widowed mother, while Matt had kept more to himself, as he always did when grief struck him, just like what he was doing now. Laura had also called him once. She had left a message, but Matt hadn't bothered to return her call.

He'd spent most of his time in his apartment sleeping, watching *Seinfeld* on DVD, petting Minerva, and eventually doing some soft research about Tikvah Zhytomyr. He had just read the organization's website and opened its Wikipedia entry. As a result, he scattered some basic annotations in his notebook and in a Word document he kept open all day. The PC monitor's fluorescent glare was the only light inside the apartment. The document read:

Tikvah Zhytomyr is a Hasidic cohort. Hasidism is a branch of Judaism that started in Eastern Europe around the middle of the 17th century. It was influenced by the teachings of Rabbi Baal Shem Tov, who was revered as a healer and even a saint by many of his devotees. Baal Shem Tov's teachings were sustained by an emphasis on the joys of life and partying combined with an unusual interest in the teachings of the Kabbalah.

The positive Hasidic approach to orthodox Judaism was especially relevant in a time and place where most Jewish communities had been decimated by killings, persecutions, and blood libels. After Baal Shem Tov passed away, his closest adepts and disciples flew across Europe to establish Hasidic cohorts where they would carry on their master's teachings.

Most of the communities were named after the place they were found. Tikvah Zhytomyr was one of those. It was started by Rabbi Joseph of Lemberg (1743-1803) in Zhytomyr, modern Ukraine. The community survived the Second World War and the communist regime.

The most prominent rabbis in Hasidic communities are commonly referred to by the honorific "rebbe." They serve as *de facto* leaders of their respective Hasidic groups.

Although Matt did not include it in the Word document, "Tikvah" in "Tikvah Zhytomyr" intrigued him. He searched an online Hebrew dictionary and learned it meant "hope." He dug deeper and discovered that Tikvah Zhytomyr's Hasidim had high hopes for the Messiah's arrival, so the name made sense. Unfortunately, there wasn't much else he could find on the Internet. He would probably need to head to a library if he would finally accept Margaret Wainstein's offer. The last thing he researched was the biographies of Tikvah Zhytomyr's six leaders. It took him a day-long reading, mainly on the group's official webpage. He had started his day eating a slice of cold pizza and a cup of coffee, reading about Joseph of Lemberg. When noon arrived, he had already reached the third generation. He arrived late that afternoon at Shmuel Abraham Josefson Bumen, the sixth and final rebbe of Tikvah Zhytomyr. In 2005, just two days after turning 100, the man died in his bed close to where Matt was at that very moment. He hadn't been replaced yet, even though over ten years had passed since his death. Under his leadership, Tikvah

Zhytomyr expanded in territorial reach and adapted to the modern world to a certain degree.

According to his web research, every Saturday afternoon, Tikvah centers in the city, known as "Tikvah Houses," hosted various activities for Jews of all ages. A Tikvah House near his apartment catered to young Jews aged eighteen to thirty-five. It held a different themed night every Saturday at seven o'clock in the afternoon. He looked at the calendar; it was Saturday for sure. He had almost lost the notion of the time he had passed keeping for himself alone and detached from the rest of the world. Why not try one of those gatherings in the Tikvah House? What did he have to lose? He got up from the chair, reached for a jacket, and got outside the apartment.

CHAPTER 8

SHAYNA

Her punishment had not been as severe as she had expected. She hadn't thought about what would happen if she left her fiancé alone in the restaurant, one of the most popular places in the Tikvah Zhytomyr community. Now that she was facing those consequences, she felt they could have been much worse.

The first hint she got she would escape almost punishment-free from her misconduct came when she arrived home immediately after leaving Mordechai Posner alone with his soul. Instead of screaming and grounding her to her room, her father had called her to his desk and, with a notoriously tired voice, had told her she was to spend the following week helping her uncle organize events for his Tikvah House. It was the fifth of the Lehrer brothers, the younger and the only one, along with Shayna's father, that still lived in the States. The others were disseminated worldwide, expanding Tikvah's teachings and trying to convince more Jews to join them.

Abraham Lehrer, Shayna's uncle, oversaw one of Tikvah's most important operations in the city, the Tikvah House for Young Jews. It was a space where Jews from eighteen to thirty-five were always welcomed to join different activities and social reunions. Every Saturday, they would host a special reunion to celebrate the end of *Shabbos,* including free meals, Jewish matchmaking, and lectures by the most charismatic rabbis from the community. For Shayna, all the outreach to secular and non-religious Jews her community did as a fundamental part of its daily work was nothing new. However, she had never taken part much in them. Shayna's status as the daughter of the great Rabbi Moshe Lehrer had put her aside most of her life.

While Shayna felt lucky that she was not being more severely punished for her misdeed, she was also lamenting having to help his uncle, which she didn't like. But she also knew there was a motive for his father to choose this form of punishment, as forcing her to help his uncle was a way to serve other Jews to encounter the truth in Tikvah Zhytomyr. It was a form of *tzedakah*, philanthropy.

Why didn't she like her uncle Abraham? She couldn't tell for sure, but maybe it was because of all the gossip about him in the community. Nothing had been proven yet, and the bad things people said about him were just hurtful rumors spread by nosy people. And that was not even something distinctive of him. Almost anyone living in the Tikvah Zhytomyr community was the object of bad faith and hurtful gossip just because that was what bored people who mainly had no interaction with the world outside their tight community would do.

One story that had spread like wildfire over the community involved the time her uncle had been as a *sheliah*, an emissary of the Rebbe, in Buenos Aires, Argentina. According to that story, Rabbi Abraham had thoughtfully turned blind eyes to some *Shabbos* dinners he had organized while developing his youth center there. The evil tongues had spread the rumor that during those dinner parties, the *frei*, secular Jews, stimulated by the free-roaming vodka, had ended in sex orgies that the rabbi had consented to or failed to stop. It was such an absurd idea that something like that had happened that Shayna never took those rumors seriously. But something about her uncle made her feel uneasy, and she couldn't put her finger on it.

Now, she had to be there and be as helpful as possible, so she tried hard to forget her natural dislike of his uncle when he greeted her. It was undoubtedly that the man was charismatic and charming, and she felt warmed by his welcoming words.

"I am so glad to have my little niece here!" he said.

"I am glad as well, uncle."

"*Baruch HaShem*! Great, many great things are coming this way!"

She smiled back.

"Could you maybe give a hand in the kitchen? I have two women doing all the cooking, but you know, they are gentiles."

She knew what his uncle was referring to. While he was confident enough in those women to do the cooking, in the end, he would be more comfortable knowing that a pair of Jewish eyes had been monitoring the process not to miss anything so that he could do the final blessings.

"I can take over the kitchen, sure."

"Great, that is why God has made the kitchen the place for women to be," he said with satisfaction.

Shayna knew that night was important for his uncle, as he was expecting a sizeable crowd. There was going to be a lecture by Rabbi Isaac Setzer from Tikvah in El Paso, Texas. He was known for gathering many people whenever he spoke in public. "Rabbi Isaac will lecture about the importance of marriage and, most of all, the importance of Jews marrying other Jews. So you might be interested in hearing him," said her uncle while showing her the way to the kitchen.

Why had he said that to her? Was this part of his father's punishment? She knew she was to marry Mordechai Posner; it was just that he had been so dull she had simply felt like leaving him during their date. But that didn't mean she would not marry him in the end. At least, that was what she tried to convince herself of.

They entered the kitchen, and her uncle clapped his hands to gain the attention of the two women cooks. They seemed Latinas, and one was older than the other, probably mother and daughter judging by how much they looked alike. "Attention, please. She is Shayna, my niece, and she will help you this afternoon. I cannot spend much time here, so all the supervision will be done by her."

The two women spoke a few words in Spanish between them and then welcomed Shayna.

"Keep a close eye on those two so that the *kashruth* is observed," her uncle said upon leaving, "with *shiksas,* you can never be sure."

She nodded courteously. Why had he hired *Goyim* if he would be so annoying about them? She had nothing against the non-Jews and never really had. But she also knew she was not in the position most of the Tikvah community held. A sense of distrust was common when referring to them. People tried to avoid interacting with anyone who was not part of the community and, especially, was not a Jew. Interacting with other Jews who were not religious was part of their mission, so they accepted it. However, some people never grew used to doing it. Shayna was neutral but curious about other people, especially about non-Jews. She couldn't conceive how people lived their lives apart from the Torah. Still, hers was more of a sense of curiosity rather than fear or a feeling of superiority like most people in Tikvah saw the rest of the world.

"Hi," she said timidly to the two women who had not stopped cooking.

"Hello," said the oldest one with a clear Spanish accent. "I am Juana. And this is my daughter, Marisa."

"Nice to meet you."

"Are you here to supervise us?" said Marisa. She was probably around Shayna's age. Still, she was much smaller than Shayna and had black, thin, short hair, while Shayna's red hair reached her shoulders.

"I wouldn't say supervise but lend you a hand."

Juana laughed. Shayna wasn't expecting that and felt a little uncomfortable.

"It is okay, *m'hija*," she said. "We have known your uncle for years, and we don't get offended by his constant supervision by now."

"Anyway, let me help you with those *knishes* you are cooking."

"Help yourself," Juana said, extending her arm to the table where the mashed potato and onion mixture was being prepared to fill small circles of flat dough.

From the lobby, many unfamiliar voices emerged, all superposed by the unmissable deep voice of Shayna's uncle. His tone was confident and outgoing. Shayna knew he was working his magic with the *frei*, trying to persuade them to do more *mitzvot* with subtle arguments and mind tricks. Everyone who had taken the mission to bring secular Jews into Tikvah Zhytomyr had developed his own method of persuasion. It was something to see. Shayna had seen much of that during her life. She had seen people more and less prepared for that delicate mission, some triumphant and many failures. Some rabbis tried very hard to be easygoing and adaptable to modern life. Still, they never quite got the spark they needed, and when they were trying to convince a hard case, they lost their cool. They were not good at all with younger *frei* but were instead very effective with broken people. People who had broken hearts, lost their money, felt spiritually overwhelmed, or had PTSD and were living on the streets, who needed rules to get their lives back on track. They were eager to accept the allowed word of an authoritative figure, like a rabbi, who told them what they had to do to regain meaning in their lives.

The young ones were the toughest. Those who had adapted best to modern life and had only had brief contact with their Jewish heritage. Young people who did not check to see if their partner was Jewish before dating, the people who had not read a single word of Hebrew, much less Yiddish, during their entire life. For them, there were people like her uncle. Those like him seemed to have been born to the job. Shayna had observed that the no-so-secret key to their success was to go one minimal, small step at a time. If they started telling a young secular Jew all the six hundred and thirteen rules that every Jew must follow, they were doomed to fail before they even started. Instead, they had to introduce the *mitzvot* one at a time, and naturally, to make them seem like something coming from themselves and not an imposition. Eventually, the right people developed a love for the Torah. Then, it was time to enforce the more obscure and difficult precepts. However simple, the method was difficult to follow, and most Jews that took part in the communal activities Tikvah pulled before getting to that point. They never became full members of the community. But even those lost causes counted. Every observed *mitzvah* counted toward making the world a more sacred place.

Her uncle Abraham had developed his abilities, judging by what she heard from the lobby. He appeared clownish in his forms of expression. However, she knew it was just a facade, that he was still a very serious rabbinical authority, and that he observed the *mitzvot*.

"Do you want to try one?" said Marisa, extending a *knish* taken just out of the oven.

"So that you can judge if we did them well," added her mother.

"Oh, as I have already told you, no need to worry about that."

"So, you don't like the way we cook?" said Juana in all seriousness.

"It is not that."

"I know! I was kidding you, *chica*," repeated the woman and burst into a laugh that made Shayna uncomfortable.

"Come here, let me taste it then," she said, grabbing the hot snack and biting it.

It was good. It tasted even better than the ones her mother usually cooked. "A Jew needs to be helped with kindness and firmness so he can find his true self and start following the rules to build the house for the Messiah on Earth." The teaching of Tikvah Zhytomyr's last Rebbe, Shmuel Abraham Josefson Bunem, came to her mind in that instant for no reason. While the study of the Torah was reserved for men, her father had made everything he could to teach her the lessons of the six Tikvah Zhytomyr's Rebbes.

"Are you feeling well?" said Marisa, holding her by the arm.

Shayna looked around the kitchen.

"You look as if we had poisoned you," said Juana, and then both mother and daughter burst into one of those laughs that made Shayna feel out of place.

"Please be assured that we did not poison it," said Marisa.

Shayna said nothing else because she didn't like that conversation and had been taught that it's better to stay quiet when you don't have anything good to say.

"Can I ask you a silly question?" said Shayna, trying to divert the conversation.

"Sure," agreed Juana.

"What does ham taste of?"

"*¿Qué dices?* What are you saying?" asked the woman, surprised.

"Just that. I have never tasted pork or ham in my life. And I am a little curious about how it tastes."

"Well, there are a bunch of different hams, you know that, right?"

"Yes, of course."

"Each of them tastes different. I wouldn't know how to describe it."

"But is it like... I don't know... chicken, for instance?"

"Not at all," said Marisa firmly. "It is tasty and salted and...."

"You should try it by yourself to know," interrupted her Juana.

The kitchen door opened, and Shayna's uncle appeared through it.

"Are those *knishes* ready yet? We have a full house tonight, and we need to give these people something, or they will leave!" said the rabbi, agitated.

Marisa took a tray full of hot *knishes* and went outside. She placed them on a table, and people immediately surrounded them and took them from the tray as if they were starving. Shayna looked at the public through the open door of the kitchen. She knew that most of them were there that night because of the promise of the "Study Trip," as his uncle called it. They had been promised a free-of-cost week trip to Israel if they agreed to participate in a year of weekly activities in the Tikvah House for Young Jews. While mostly all of them took it as a chance for a free flight to another exotic country, the trip was a strictly religious pilgrimage. But, of course, that was not explicitly disclosed. Not only were the travelers separated by sex once they arrived in Israel, but the stops in the country were all of Jewish religious significance. Travel included visits to Jerusalem's orthodox Mea Sharim neighborhood and Western Wall, Safed to see the tomb of Rabbi Isaac Luria and other significant locations for Tikvah Zhytomyr.

The rabbi went once again into the kitchen. "Shayna, I need you to help at the reception. We are having more public than we expected tonight."

Shayna followed her uncle to the front door, where she saw Melanie, a girl she had known before and never quite liked. It was because she was the right hand of her uncle, or maybe because of something else that she couldn't quite grasp. The most likely reason was that she was a *ba'al teshuva*, or "returner." This meant that she was a former secular Jew who had turned to follow Jewish law the way Tikvah Zhytomyr taught it. As any recent convert, she was especially inquisitorial and even a little obsessed about how others in the community behaved. Shayna suspected she had told her uncle about some of her minor transgressions to Jewish laws and customs on some occasions.

"My uncle told me you need my help," said Shayna coldly.

Melanie's disgust at the sight of her was clear and unmasked.

"I can take care alone, but if he asked you to be here, he might have had his reasons. So, you can pick up those inscription forms and go around the people in the line asking them to complete them. The conference by Rabbi Setzer has proven much more popular than we first thought it would be."

About that, she was right. A long line formed that even reached the outside of the place. Shayna took a pile of inscription forms and started going down the line, asking people to fill them out.

"Excuse me," said one voice, "this is my first time attending one of these events, and I am not completely sure what I am expected to do."

Shayna looked up tiredly and saw a young man standing in front of her with an ironic smile on his face.

"As I was telling you," said the guy, "I am not sure what I am supposed to do or what form I have to fill."

"Sure, no problem. Let's see," said Shayna, marking a star of David in the field that said "Mother's last name" in one form.

"So, this is what matters most. Please don't tell anyone I told you this is the only thing that matters. So the big question is, 'Is your mom Jewish?'"

"Mom?" asked the guy. "Um, yes. Why?"

"Nothing special," said Shayna. She knew that if his mother weren't Jewish, one of those big, ugly security guards would ask him to leave.

"So, you just put your information here, and that's it."

"Nothing else?"

"Well, you can tell me your name," Shayna said, realizing she was being flirtatious without even intending, "so that I can catch up with you later," she added, "and see if you need any more help."

"Seems fair. My name is Matthew. People call me Matt," said the guy as he extended his hand.

"I am Shayna; nice to meet you," answered her, ignoring his extended hand and continuing down the line, giving the forms to the people formed.

That had been something new for her. She had been used to talking to the same few men from her family and some others from the community, but this felt like the time she had been to that bar at midnight. Audacious and incorrect. And also exciting.

When she ran out of forms, she returned to the reception desk. The conference was about to start, and there were still plenty of people trying to get in.

"Many people today," she said, trying to start a friendly conversation with Melanie. She was feeling in a better mood now.

"Yeah. Here, please help me organize all these filled forms."

"Is it always like this when there is a special conference?"

"Yeah, well, not as much as today."

"And how long does Rabbi Setzer stay when he visits here?"

"What? How do I know?" said Melanie, annoyed.

A silence grew between the two girls.

"I am sorry," said Melanie, acknowledging that it probably wasn't a good idea to go head-to-head with the daughter of Rabbi Moshe Lehrer

"I was so focused on getting all the information from the forms to the computer that your questions made me nervous."

"Don't worry about it."

Melanie kept processing the forms while Shayna felt she had accomplished a minor triumph with that showdown. She had gained at least a few inches of impunity. Shayna went through all the forms until she found the one with the star of David in her handwriting next to the "mother's last name" placeholder. She copied Matt's name, last name, and phone number into a piece of paper that she quickly put in her skirt pocket, full of anxiety and guilty feelings.

CHAPTER 9

MATT

He was surprised to see so many more people than he had expected. The door was almost hidden, surrounded by gentrified bars and designer apparel stores. The line extended, taking over almost half the street. It seemed to him like one hundred persons were waiting just to enter the place. At first glance, he could tell that most people were probably in their thirties. Based on what he could overhear, most of them were there to take advantage of an offer of a free trip to Israel.

Although the queue was significant, it moved fast, and he could get inside just half an hour after arriving. He passed through the modest door to a big lobby surrounded by red-colored walls full of posters that promoted some events and weekly activities. There was a mix of everything: *Kabbalah for Beginners; Getting to Know Your Jewish Heritage; The Bubbe's Cookbook; Everything You Ever Wanted to Know About the Coming of the Messiah But You Were Too Afraid to Ask.* Every seminar, as they were called, was explained with a brief, sometimes fun paragraph below the title and a photograph. Matt thought the cooking one might even be useful for him because he never knew what to cook for himself, let alone for any guests he might have at home from time to time. At the back of the hall, high on the wall, was a large portrait of an old man in black with a long curly beard streaked with gray hair. He recognized Shmuel Abraham Josefson Bunem, Zhytomyr's last rebbe in the oil painting. During the last few days, he had spent a lot of time reading about his life and times along with the lives of previous Zhytomyr's rebbes.

At the end of that hallway, and before passing a door, there was a reception desk. Matt could see that there was still a long line ahead of him and another long line that had formed behind him. A redhead girl in a simple shirt that covered her neck and a long, deep blue skirt that went up to her ankles was walking through the line, handing out forms to those in attendance. She looked only 19 or 20 years old and moved through the line like a robot, never taking her eyes off the floor. She passed by him, handled the form, and was back on her way when he stopped her to ask for some indications. When the girl finally looked up, he realized she was even more stunning than he had imagined. She had blue eyes and a delicate, freckled face. With her help, he completed the form and later handed it to the receptionist. He was finally granted access to Tikvah House for Young Jews.

The interior was packed with people, mostly in their early 30s. As they formed small groups scattered around the room, it appeared that most of them already knew each other. A charismatic man dressed in black from his toes to his fur hat walked around, calling out everyone's name, hugging some men, and treating the women with contemplative respect. Matt started to feel like he didn't belong like he'd been invited to a birthday party where everyone already knew each other. He approached a big table in the middle of the living room full of sodas, *knishes,* and petite pastrami sandwiches, poured himself a glass of Coke, and grabbed a sandwich. He was about to take his first bite when he heard a voice behind him.

"Did you know Coke is kasher?"

He turned around.

"I'm sorry if I caught you off guard! I wasn't trying to scare you. You can keep eating and drinking if you want to. My name is Abraham Lehrer, and this is my *shule*, a place for young Jews who want to learn about their history, traditions, and heritage."

Matt left the glass and the sandwich on the table.

"Nice to meet you. I am Matthew."

The rabi extended his hand.

"I am glad that you are here with us tonight. We will have a magnificent lecture by my friend, Rabbi Setzer."

"That is great."

"Well, I will let you enjoy the food and the company. I'll be around if you need anything."

"Sure."

The rabbi was turning to continue welcoming the new arrivals when Matt stopped him.

"I am sorry, rabbi...."

"Yes?"

"It is only that I didn't give you a chance to explain all that about Coke being kasher, and I must admit that now I am a little intrigued."

"Aren't you? That is one surprise getting to know Judaism gives you! I know! It is crazy! A fascinating story."

"Well, yes. The thing is that I have never been very interested in my Jewish roots. And now that I am here...."

"There is a reason you are here. Maybe you won't believe me now, but *HaShem* has a reason for everything he does. So, let us return to the KasCoke thing, shall we? It started in nineteen thirty-five. Hold on! I know what you probably think: 'Ugh, another boring history class? I didn't sign up for this!' Just give me a second; you will see this is unlike a high-school history class. So, the year I have told you, the man was Tuvia Geffen, a rabbi who lived in Atlanta. His community tasked him with certifying that Coke was kasher because, you know, everybody wanted to drink it, and if it wasn't, they couldn't. So he went to the production plant and certified it. And you might be thinking, 'What is this *meshugheneh* talking about? Nobody knows Coke's secret formula! It would have been impossible for anyone to certify that it is kasher!' Well, Rabbi Geffen was exceptionally granted permission to know the secret ingredients under oath of never revealing it to the world. And he stayed true to that oath. I know what you are thinking: 'Now this rabbi is taking me for a *meshugheneh*! There is no way his story could be true as there is no sign on the Coke label it is kasher!' And you would be correct. There is not. But that has to do with Coke's marketing decisions."

Matt had not imagined his first interaction with Tikvah Zhytomyr would be about whether Coke was kosher, but that was exactly what had occurred.

"Let me add one more thing to this amazing story, and then I will leave you to enjoy the food and kasherCoke. In a few weeks, you might see some Coke bottles with yellow caps instead of the usual red ones. Well, a yellow Coke cap means it can be drunk during Passover. This is because we, Jews, do not ingest any *kitniyot* during that time. This is legumes and grains like corn. Usually, Coke is made with high fructose corn syrup. For this time of year, though, small batches of Coke are made with sugar instead of corn syrup so that we can still drink it during the days of Passover. Fascinating, don't you think?"

Matt thought it was more of a curiosity than a fascinating fact, but he nodded either way.

"Well, this is also part of your heritage as a Jew. Now you know it. I will now leave you alone so that you can enjoy the food and socialize. And please, don't miss the lecture by Rabbi Setzer. It will blow your mind. I am sure."

He then gave him a pat on the shoulder and went to talk to some of the other assistants, who were happy to see him again.

Matt looked back at his glass, trying to find something unique about that Coke that wasn't like any other Coke. He started to feel stupid as if a snake oil salesman had tricked him. He looked around; there were many men and women, teenagers and young people, and they all seemed to be having a good time talking to one another. He knew some love stories, marriages, and children would eventually be born from those gatherings. After the accident, something like that happened to his friend David. This was *Rabbi's Lehrer Lonely Hearts Club*.

After some time, people started pouring into another bigger lounge with lines of seats arranged in front of a sleek-looking white leather three-seater couch. A set of blue lights from the sides trickled in the middle of the room, just over the couch, making it central stage. Matt did what everyone else did and sat in the first row. When Rabbi Lehrer walked on stage, everyone fell silent.

"*Shalom*, good evening to all of you, and thank you for being here!" he said enthusiastically. "Today, we are honored to have here with us Rabbi Isaac Setzer, who has come all the way from his small Tikvah House in El Paso, Texas, to us! If, for any reason, you need to go to El Paso, you now know that you will have a Jewish friend in Rabbi Setzer down there! Surprised yet? Why? Are you asking yourself how Tikvah is present in places with such small Jewish populations? So, as we say in Tikvah, 'wherever there is a Jew, there we will be.' And it is true. It is true. Please join me in applause to welcome Rabbi Isaac Setzer!"

Hands clapped, and a tall, thin man wearing all black appeared from the side. He walked through the rows of seats, giving high fives to some people, and then gave Rabbi Lehrer a firm hug before sitting in the middle of the white couch with him.

"*Baruch HaShem*! Thank you for your warm welcome! First, I would like to thank my friend, Rabbi Abraham, for inviting me tonight to this special occasion. I feel honored." He addressed the public. "I know most of you are here because this Tikvah House has a great study program. But let's be honest, I don't fool myself, and I don't think anyone else does either. We all know that most of you are here for the 'dessert,' which is the trip to Israel you will take once the course is completed."

Some nervous giggles rose from the public.

"It is fine. It is completely fine! It will be a well-deserved prize for your engagement in the program. Here in Tikvah, we think of Jews as empty vessels, and our mission is to fill that emptiness with substance."

The public went silent in expectation.

"Fill you with substance. Get it? Now you can laugh." Some scattered laughs were heard. "Well, let's cut to the chase then, shall we? Why am I here tonight? To talk to you about something fundamental, I would say, I know some of you will find it controversial. What is this? The holiness of marriage and the importance of marrying another Jew."

Murmurs started, and Rabbi Setzer got up from the couch and walked around the stage.

"I knew this topic would interest you," he stated. "So, without passing judgment, how many men here currently date a non-Jew woman?"

Murmurs became louder, but no one dared respond directly to him.

"Come on! Men who are dating non-Jews among you, raise your hands! Rest assured that no one will take away the trip to Israel from you!"

Some hands rose timidly. Then others followed, and finally, about a quarter of the men present had raised their hands, including Matt.

"*Oi vey*!" said the rabbi, touching his forehead. "Much more than I expected, Abraham!"

"I warned you they are a tough public," responded Rabbi Lehrer.

"Let's move on. Now I would like to know which of you are not dating anyone right now but have dated a gentile in the past."

About half of the total public raised their hands.

"I see," said Rabbi Setzer, disappointed. "No wonder we are experiencing right now a Silent Holocaust. What is that? I will explain. Give me a second so that I can recover myself. By the way, can I have a glass of Coke?"

Marisa, the girl from the kitchen, appeared from the side carrying a tray with a glass of Coke.

"Great, thank you," greeted the rabbi. "You all know that Coke is kasher, right? What am I asking? Rabbi Lehrer has probably already told you this story if you're here. So, let's move on. What is that Silent Holocaust I was talking about before? Well, it is simply finishing the Nazi's work. The result will be the same, the extinction of our people. This time, they don't need the gas chambers! It is easier for them! They will reassure you it is perfectly acceptable for you to wed a non-Jew or a gentile. Some will even tell you you should have as many children as possible with that gentile. This way, they guarantee that in the short run, we Jews will cease to exist. If we start having children with non-Jews, we are going extinct. Do you know who would be happy about this? Adolf Hitler himself. He would say, 'These Jews are more stupid than I first thought! They are now exterminating themselves with their interfaith marriages!' It is like that. Absolutely. Interfaith marriages are the new gas chambers. If one of you, a Jewish man, marries a gentile and has children with her, those children will not be part of the Jewish people. It's that plain. Those two, three, or four children you'll have with that goy woman will be two, three, or four Jewish children fewer in the world."

Matt's phone vibrated in his pocket. He took it out. Laura had sent him a message.

want to hang up?

He thought he had enough to pen a report for Margaret Wainstein, cash the cheque, and move on.

in an hour at my place

He wrote back to Laura just when the rabbi was finishing his speech. Most people had stood up and returned to the living room, where some went straight back to the large table, which was now laden with desserts. Matt headed to the exit.

"What a bore, right?" he heard someone saying to him.

He looked back. A good-looking blond girl around his age was looking at him.

"Sorry, are you talking to me?"

"Yeah. Just saying."

"No, you are right. It was dull."

"It gets worse every time."

"You have been here before?"

"It is my third attempt to finish the course. I want to get that free trip, but it is so incredibly tiresome to stand for the entire year of the course. This time, I have decided it will be my last attempt. Either I make it, or I will move on."

"Well, I better get going. Nice to meet you...."

"Denise."

"My name's Matt. Do you want to give me your number so we can attend together next time?"

The blond girl seemed to evaluate the idea for a few seconds.

"Sure. Have my number," she said and dictated it to him.

"Until next time, then." He said.

"Sure."

He stepped out onto the street and felt the breeze on his face.

CHAPTER 10

MATT

He walked a block aimlessly, trying hard to understand what was going on in his mind. Before that night, he had imagined what the capture mechanism would be like. He knew they would not be able to mess with his head. Still, the sum of the euphoria, the food, the friendly chat with the rabbi, and the mix of men and women in ebullition had stunned him. He kept walking straight ahead until he came across another Tikvah Center; he had the locations of nearby Tikvah centers marked on Google Maps. He had never seen such a mix of modern consumerism and extreme conservatism before. He was still trying to figure it out. The worst part was that he felt something deep in his Jewish roots had come to the surface that night. It was as if he had been drugged and inducted into a sect or a cult. He had left just before it could take total control over his brain. But it was still there, floating like a thick fog around him, and he could even see it in the neighborhood where he was now walking. It hadn't been like that until recently. Now, it seemed like Tikvah Zhytomyr had taken it over. Plenty of new kasher restaurants and stores selling Jewish books, and Hasidic men and women walked the streets and around him, going on with their lives. At the same time, he struggled to grasp why David embraced that lifestyle. It suddenly became a little more transparent.

He entered his apartment and was received by Minerva, standing at the center of the room. It hadn't passed five seconds when he heard the buzzer ringing. It was Laura, and she was waiting downstairs. He returned and opened the door for her, who stamped her lips on his without saying a word. Matt wasn't expecting that.

"Whoa! Hello to you, too."

"Shut up and kiss me," she ordered.

What was happening to her? She rarely showed her feelings straightforwardly.

"Is everything fine?"

"Yes, sure. Why do you ask?"

"I don't know."

"So, will you let me in, or will we spend the night here?"

They climbed the stairs back to his apartment. Upon entering, she pushed him to the bed and took off her shirt. He followed her. They made love with a newfound sense of urgency and passion. All the mixed feelings, anguish, and almost the entire last week were suddenly lost for Matt. This was his life, his real life. It didn't involve charismatic Hasidic rabbis, trips to a country he had never cared much about, or anything in between. His life was of a young man trying to make it in the city with an English degree, dating a woman around his age who was probably above his league. And that was fine. Totally fine.

"Do you have a smoke?" said Laura.

"I am trying to quit. I have flushed the ones I had remaining. But I can offer you some weed."

"Sure."

Matt got out of bed, changed into his underwear, and reached into his stash for a pre-rolled joint.

They smoked together in bed.

"Is it okay if I spend the night here?"

"Yes," he said, trying to hide that her asking had surprised him.

His phone rang. It was nearly midnight.

"Who is calling you at this hour?" asked Laura, annoyed.

"I do not know. Maybe my brother. I won't pick it. They can call me again tomorrow."

The phone stopped ringing, and then it started again.

"Just pick it up," said Laura.

Matt stretched from the bed and took it. The caller had already hung up. He had two missed calls. The screen read "Unknown number."

CHAPTER 11

SHAYNA

"What a mess," said Shayna, looking around the now-empty Tikvah House for Young Jews. Piles of empty plates, food waste all over the table, and spilled Coke made for a depressing view.

"It always is like this after the meetings," said Juana.

"Well, you don't always have me to lend you a hand with the cleaning."

Juana then murmured something that Shayna couldn't hear. Nobody had asked her to stay and help, but she thought not doing it would be rude. So there she was, armed with a dust mop and trying to help without being invasive. Her uncle, Rabbi Abraham, was now having a relaxed meeting with his friend Isaac in his office. They were drinking vodka and laughing; even some Yiddish curse words could also be heard coming that way. "Look for the good, not the evil, in the conduct of family members." The Yiddish proverb came to her mind while mopping the floor and hearing what the two men were shouting.

Melanie completed the paperwork, shut down her computer, and went to the office where the two rabbis were at a meeting to inform them she was leaving for the night. They barely noticed her, waved their hands, and continued their animated conversation. She then passed through where Shayna, Marisa, and Juana were working, coldly said goodbye, and got out.

"*Esa pinche gringa la tiene bien fácil*," said Juana, and Marisa laughed.

Shayna stared at her for a moment.

"I am sorry, *m'hija*. I was saying that the other girl isn't as committed as you are."

"Oh, don't worry about me. By the way, does she always leave before everything is cleaned up?"

"Every time," said Marisa.

"Maybe it is because she is not like us," added Juana.

"What do you mean?"

"I mean, she is like you. Not like Marisa and me. She is one of your kind."

Shayna felt like her blood was suddenly going through her head.

"I am of my kind and still here," she said.

"You could leave if you wanted," said Marisa.

Shayna felt like she was being challenged. So be it, then.

"You know what? You are right. I am leaving," she said, putting the mop against a wall. She then went through her uncle's office and asked him if there was anything else he needed from her.

"My dear Shayna!" said Rabbi Abraham with a humorous tone. "Come here, dear niece. Close the door behind you. Let's chat a little."

Shayna wasn't expecting that. She would not close the door. It was against the rules for her to be alone in a room with two men. She entered and leaned against a wall in the corner.

"How was your afternoon?"

"Fine."

"I hope you didn't mix too much with those *shiksas*. I saw you around them," added Rabbi Setzer.

"Only as much as was necessary."

Her uncle got up from his executive chair and walked until he got in front of her. He then surrounded her with extended arms; his hands pressed against the wall at her sides.

"Please, uncle, you are making me uncomfortable," said Shayna.

Her uncle's face gained a twisted smile, and then he slowly traced a line with one of his fingers on Shayna's face until reaching her chin.

"What are you doing? You are touching me."

"Come on, Shayna! It is kasher! We are family! It is allowed."

Shayna knew perfectly well that it was not. Only a father could have physical contact with his daughter; even those contacts had to be limited and follow specific rules.

She moved her head away from her uncle's finger, and a tense silence gained the room for some seconds. Then, Rabbi Lehrer burst into a laugh, followed by a similar laugh by Rabbi Setzer.

Her uncle went back to his executive chair.

"Shayna is a little uneasy these days," he told his friend. "She's been through a lot recently."

Rabbi Setzer changed his facial expression.

"Such a disgrace, Shayna. I know that there are certain things your father prefers not to talk about, and it will not be me who contradicts his will. But I still want you to know I am very sorry about what happened. I can't imagine what you are going through," he said solemnly.

Shayna thought about her sister for the first time in weeks. It was certainly the first time someone in the Tikvah community mentioned Chaia to her. It felt good for a moment. But then she saw the twisted grin on her uncle's face again and felt frightened.

"So, what were you saying, my beloved niece?"

"Just that I have already finished my duties and am heading home."

Her uncle smiled and raised his hands over his shoulders.

"You are the daughter of Moshe Lehrer, right hand of our rebbe. We might even say, a *tzaddiq*! You don't need my permission to get out of here. You can do as you please! You are holly!"

Shayna noticed the ironic tone with which her uncle had said that but ignored it.

"This is your house," she answered. "I don't want to be impolite."

"Nothing to worry about. You can go. Thank you for being so helpful tonight."

"*Shalom,*" said Shayna and left the office. She was one step out when she heard the voice of Rabbi Setzer on her back.

"Shayna, just one moment before you leave," he said.

She just stood there, facing away from the two men.

"Yes?"

"Don't you think there was something... how do you say... sketchy about how your sister died?"

Shayna didn't answer. A single tear dropped from his left eye.

Setzer said, "I mean, dying because of your own will is a terrible sin. Not only that, but the horrible way she died... crucified as the false Messiah... and what she and her husband did to their children. I can't imagine."

She turned around to face the men again.

"You know," she said, "I didn't get to know my sister very well."

"That's just not true," said her uncle, "but, hey, it is not me who will contradict the daughter of a *tzaddiq*! One last thing, before you go," he added, "have you ever heard of blood libels?"

Shayna took a moment to think. It didn't sound like anything she might have known.

"I don't think so," she finally said. "Am I supposed to know?"

"Not at all. You shouldn't get mixed with those things. They are a truly horrible matter. Anyway, go now and please don't ask my brother about this or anything related. He has enough going on, and everybody knows he is not so prone to talk about his dead daughter."

Shayna had had enough of those men and was now ready to leave.

"You know how the Yiddish proverb goes: parents can give everything but common sense," she said before leaving the room.

Rabbi Setzer smiled.

"There is truth in the words of our sages."

"Now, if you excuse me," said Shayna, finally leaving the place without saying a word to the women still cleaning as she passed them.

She returned home and went straight to bed. She had some disturbing dreams that night.

CHAPTER 12

MATT

It was ten past eleven in the morning. Laura had left an hour ago, and he was again alone with his thoughts. He was writing down some thoughts he had after attending the Tikvah House for Young Jews event when his phone started to ring. He stretched his arm to catch it and saw again the "Unknown number" glaring on the screen. This time, he answered before the caller hung up.

"Is this Matt?"

"Yes, with whom am I speaking?"

"This is Shayna,"

"Shayna?"

"We met yesterday at the event at the Tikvah House."

He remembered the blond girl he had briefly chatted with after the lecture by the rabbi.

"Oh yeah, I remember you! You are the girl fed up with the Hasidim but still wanted the trip to Israel."

There was a brief silence from the other side of the line.

"I think you got me wrong. I am Shayna. I took your personal information when you were standing in line to get in."

Matt went back in his head to the situation and then remembered. This one was the ginger girl. And she was one of them.

"I am so sorry I have mistaken you for another person," he tried to excuse himself. "I don't think you told me your name, thus the confusion. So, how are you doing, Shayna?"

"*Baruch HaShem*, I am fine. I am calling you to invite you to our Purim festival. It is going to be a great time, and it is going to take place on the following Wednesday. So if you had a good time yesterday, I am sure you will also enjoy this."

Matt had decided that he had seen and read enough to fill the report for Margaret Wainstein and let everything go for once. Still, he definitely could make one further incursion into Tikvah. Why not?

"Are you coming then?"

"I suppose I could."

"That is great. Don't forget to come in a costume. Purim is like the Jewish Halloween."

"I didn't know that. I don't think I have a costume. And *Spirit* will not pop up until October."

"You can come either way. It is not compulsory to wear a costume."

"Well, in that case...."

"See you there then. We will be honored to have you."

Matt was going to say goodbye, but she had already hung up.

"These guys sure make it for the personalized experience," he thought.

Minerva woke up from one of her naps and went to him, rubbing her face against his left foot. He went to the kitchen, grabbed her food bag, and poured some into her bowl.

"Thank God you don't ask me for kasher food," he told the cat that ignored him.

His phone rang again. This time, he saw the name of his brother on the screen. He doubted taking the call but then decided that if not, it would become worse later.

Mike was in a good mood and asked if he wanted to go out for lunch.

"I assume you haven't had launch yet."

"Your assumption is correct. I had a late breakfast."

"I wonder why. Anyway, can you make it at twelve-thirty at Masaki? I am feeling like having sushi."

"You always feel like having sushi. Fine, I will meet you there."

When he got to the restaurant, his brother was sitting at a patio table. It was a cold, gray day, but nothing could interfere with Mike's passion for outdoor dining. He was talking on the phone when Matt arrived and took a seat.

"Okay, okay. Let's talk later because I have a meeting now. Bye."

Mike left his phone on the table and looked at his brother.

"Look at you. All fancy dressed and showered!"

"This?" said Matt, pointing to his polo t-shirt. "Are you kidding me?"

"Of course I am. So, how are things going in your life?"

"Fine."

"Good to hear. I was worried about you after our last meeting."

"I thought you only cared because momma was worried."

Mike sighed.

"I also care about you."

"That's good to know."

Matt didn't know how to interact with his brother. They were complete opposites.

"So... Have you seen last night's game?"

"The Blue Sox played?"

"That is not even a real team."

"You know, I don't care much about sports."

"Yeah, right," said Mike, moving his eyesight to the street. "I have already ordered, by the way. They take their time to bring the order, so I thought...."

"You thought what I would like to eat was unimportant?"

"No, I mean, well, it is just that I have to get back home in an hour, so...."

"It is fine by me. Don't worry."

"Are you sure?"

"Yeah," said Matt, although he didn't mean it. Or maybe yes. He wasn't even sure if he was bothered by how his brother always tried to take control of situations.

"So, how are Karen and the girls doing?" he asked to fill the uncomfortable silence that had grown between them.

"They are fine. I think. I don't know. I might get a divorce."

"What?"

"Nothing. Forget what I told you."

"Are you sure?"

"It is... just that things have not been great lately. I don't know. I have reached my peak in life, haven't I? I have a wife, two beautiful children, and one of the best jobs I could ever aspire to...."

"And so you are getting bored."

"I don't know. Maybe. I can't say I haven't felt I could sleep with any woman I want. And being married and being a father is not easy."

"I can imagine."

"No, you don't. Look, Matt, please take my advice and never get married."

That was a piece of advice he hadn't expected from his brother.

"I wasn't thinking about getting married, anyway."

"You told me you were seeing a gal."

"Laura. Yes. I like her. I am not sure what she feels about me. Sometimes she is cold as ice, and next time she is candid and warm and wants to sleep with me and won't leave my house until late."

"When that happens, that's your warning call."

A waitress brought the sushi and left it on the table.

"You see? That girl. My god. I really wish I could ask her out."

"But you are married and have a family."

"Now you understand."

Matt thought about Denise, the blond girl he had met at Tikvah's event, and then of the other girl, the ginger that had called to invite him to another event. And then he went back in his head to Laura. What did he feel for her? He wasn't sure.

"Are you working on something?" asked Mike.

Matt started to tell him about the research he was doing about Tikvah for Margaret Wainstein.

"Haven't you had enough of that crap?"

"What do you mean?"

"I mean... I don't want to open the paper on a Saturday and find that you have blown your brains."

"You are being unfair."

"I don't think so! What happened to the son of that poor woman you are now taking advantage of speaks for itself," said Mike, putting a piece of sushi in his open mouth.

"First, I am not taking advantage of anyone. It was she who asked me to take care of this thing. Second, you are being incredibly racist."

"No, I am not! So tell me, how is it that I am being racist for pointing out the obvious?"

"Precisely because of that. You think that just because I hang out with Orthodox Jews, I'll become crazy, suicidal, or even a cold-blooded killer?"

"Well, that happened to your friend and his family, didn't it?"

"Religion has nothing to do with what happened."

"That you don't know."

Matt thought about that and didn't answer. He didn't know if David had developed a mental condition following the accident. They had stopped talking and seeing each other when he had joined Tikvah Zhytomyr.

"There are thousands, even millions, of orthodox Jews, and you don't read in the news that they all have become murderers. Assuming that because there was one case, all of them are involved in some conspiracy is simply an antisemitic talking point. And may I remember you that you are also half-Jew?"

"Look, Matt, I don't care where you put yourself in as long as it doesn't break Mom's heart."

"Then you have nothing to worry about."

"Do what you want, but stay away from my family while hanging with these crazy people."

"Once again, you are being silly."

"I am doing what I have to protect my family."

"The same family you just said five minutes ago you wish you hadn't?"

"Don't do the wisecrack act on me."

Mike's phone rang. He looked at the screen.

"Excuse me, I have to take this call," he said and took his phone, got up, and went to talk away from the table.

Matt had imagined that outcome. It was always the same with his brother. When Mike returned to the table, he was ready to get up and go.

"Everything's fine?"

"Yeah, just something I had to take care of. Anyway, going back to what we were saying, I mean you well. I don't want you to end up in a dangerous place. That is all."

"I know."

"I will never understand what fascinates you about human behavior. You could leave your dead friend where it is and his mother to hire another guy to stick his nose into what went wrong with him."

"Besides my genuine interest in human behavior, as you noted, David was my friend. And there is also the money his mother is paying me for doing this. I am almost finished, by the way. I am only attending one more event, and that will be it."

"You could just leave it where it is, then."

"Yes, but there was this girl I met...."

"I thought you were already seeing someone right now."

"As you said, I may not want to go much further in my relationship with Laura."

Mike seemed to think for a few seconds.

"Okay, that's it. You convinced me. You will be fine and not do any stupid thing."

"That's it? I convinced just like that?" said Matt, somehow disappointed.

"Yep, that's it."

"So, you are not worried anymore that I might commit crazy acts like David."

"David was an idiot."

"And I am not?"

"You are many things, brother. But an idiot, you are not. So, what are you having for dessert?"

CHAPTER 13

MATT

The Tikvah House for Young Jews looked different this time, as it had been decorated with Caribbean motives. A big sign at the reception read "Caribbean Style Purim!" and showed a picture of crystal waters surrounded by a blue sky and palm trees in the sand. Displayed in the picture were open coconuts, with straws coming out of them and baskets full of fresh fruits surrounded by candles. It seemed a little odd to him at first glance. Still, he remembered what Shayna had told him over the phone that Purim was supposed to be a kind of Jewish Halloween festival of sorts. It seemed more like a carnival to him, with all the tropical flare and, yes, people coming and going in costumes. Also, there were more people than the last time he had been there. As soon as he set foot inside, he was welcomed by an array of pirates, sirens, nurses, exotic dancers, police officers, some *Batmen*, and at least one *Winnie the Pooh*.

The host, Rabbi Abraham Lehrer, wore a Robin Hood costume and excitedly welcomed each guest.

This time, it had been easier to sneak in for Matt. He had just told his name to the receptionist, which was not the same as that was the last time. He had already been whitelisted, probably by Shayna.

He had read a lot about the Hasidic approach to tradition, and now he was finally understanding it. The same people who wore only black in mourning for losing Salomon's Second Temple over two thousand years ago were also a joyful bunch who embraced party and celebration as their theology.

The large table where they typically served food was covered with empty wine bottles. Some carnival games had been set up in the salon where Rabbi Setzer had lectured on the importance of Jews marrying other Jews the other night. The games included "Pin the Tail on the Donkey," where Queen Esther was the donkey, and the tail was a crown that the players had to pin to her head, and a shoot-the-blank game with the figure of the evil

Haman, the enemy of the Jewish people during the events of Purim, instead of ducks. There was also a fishing game in which the fish were replaced by Jews who had to be saved from King Ahasuerus's plan to kill them all.

"They do this thing every year. When you play these games, you can win fake coins, and the person who has the most at the end of the festival will get a surprise prize on the trip to Israel." Someone had just figured out what he was thinking and answered his questions about why the games were happening. He looked behind his back. Denise was standing there, costumed as Marilyn Monroe.

"I thought I would never see you again here. You didn't call me to tell me you were coming."

"I honestly didn't think I would be back, either."

"Glad you changed your mind."

"So, is the prize for winning most of those fake coins any good?" he said.

The girl took one fake coin and showed it to him. It had the face of Tikvah's last rebbe impressed on it.

"Do you think anything interesting can come from a hundred of these faces?"

"Not really, but who knows? Anyway, how many have you won so far tonight?"

"Not much. The party has just started. However, you can get five complimentary tickets just for attending. There, that guy is handling them. Ask for yours with the ticket they gave you when you arrived."

Matt reached the guy at the front door, who gave him five rebbe coins.

"Now what?" he asked Denise.

"Now we can start playing. What would you like to try first?"

Was she flirting with him? He kind of liked her, but he was unsure if he liked her as much as to betray Laura.

"What about this?" he said, pointing to a shoot-the-blank booth.

"Yeah, why not?" said Denise.

He exchanged two of his coins for a set of five darts, and they shot the figure of the evil Haman. He took his chance first and erred two of the darts. Denise took two more shots, but neither hit the target, even though they were closer to the blank.

"You take the last one," he said.

She took the last dart from Matt's hand and concentrated on the blank. Then, again, she shot; this time, the dart went through exactly Haman's figurehead.

They were rewarded with twelve rebbe coins.

"Well, that was unexpected," said Matt.

"I have been attending these festivals for some time now. My accuracy is finally catching up. Come, let's get something to drink." Denise grabbed his hand and pushed him to a bar tap that wasn't there the last time he attended.

Many people crowded around the bar, but she could still get them to the front in less than a minute. They got a beer in a plastic glass and returned to the main hall.

"Are all these people helping here today, Hasidim?"

Denise thought a little while drinking from her plastic glass.

"To be honest, this is the first time I see their faces. It seems like Rabbi Lehrer has brought some new people."

"I feel a little amazed that all this, the alcohol, the party, everything is... just free."

"It is not free. Not at all. You are paying with your soul!" said Denise, bursting into laughter. "With the dough these guys make, throwing a party like this amounts to pennies for them."

"What do you mean?"

"These are rich guys. The other day, I saw Rabbi Lehrer leaving the place in an Audi."

"The rabbi goes by in an Audi?"

"What do you think? That they were Franciscans? They make a lot of money out of fundraising. They sell these old rich Jews that the future of the Jewish people is at peril and that they are the only ones fighting for the Jewish soul and all that crap."

"And it works?"

"I can promise you that there are plenty of rich Jews dying in this city alone, let alone the rest of the country and the world, who would gladly give any of these guys money after a brief conversation. And for the tough sales, they bring Rabbi Moshe Lehrer. He can get any wallet on the fence to fully open. But enough about that. Why don't we get to a more comfortable place?"

"What are you thinking?"

"There is a couch over there, for starters."

The couch was empty and a little away from all the people drinking, talking, and playing games in all effervescence. They took a seat and looked at each other for a second. Then Denise went for his lips, and they made out. Her hands went underneath his shirt, touching him with passion.

"Do you want to go to my place?" she asked.

Matt thought that was a little too early for that.

"Later."

"Sure."

A tall, thin figure stared at them.

"Rabbi Setzer!" said Denise.

"*Shalom*, my friends, "answered the rabbi. His costume was like Rabbi Lehrer's, but instead of green, he was wearing all black.

"What are you disguised as?" asked him Denise.

"Isn't it obvious? I am the Sheriff of Nottingham!"

"Oh, I see," said Matt. "You and Rabbi Lehrer complement each other."

"Wise observation," said Setzer. "I am glad that two young Jews like yourselves are getting to know each other. I will continue guarding the premises," he said and left.

"That was slightly embarrassing on his part," said Matt.

"Yeah."

Their moment had cooled off, and now Matt regretted not accepting Denise's invitation to her place.

"Look, there, Molly," she said. "She's a friend of mine. She is not a Jew, but I got her in here all the same." She pointed to a girl around her thirties who was not wearing a costume.

Denise called her friend, who went to meet them.

The two girls hugged.

"So, this is Matt. He is new here."

"Nice to meet you, Matt."

"Nice to meet you, too. Now, seeing you, I am a little less concerned about not wearing a costume myself."

"Ugh, that stupid thing about the costume. Bring the free beer and shut up! That is what I say."

"Yeah," agreed Denise. "Speaking of which, I could do another beer."

"Great idea," said Molly, and the two girls took off to the bar.

Matt became more comfortable on the couch, looked at the ceiling, and sighed.

"You were left alone," said a female voice.

He looked at the girl. She was wearing a mask, and it took him a moment to recognize the long red-haired ponytail.

"Hi Shayna, I was wondering if I would see you here at all or if I would even recognize you. There are lots of people tonight."

"I am glad you could recognize me. And also that you remembered my name."

"Haven't you called to invite me to come?"

"Yes."

"That is why I am here."

"And what about the girl you were with?"

"What about her?"

"I don't know, you tell me. Is she your girlfriend?"

"No, not at all. We just met here. Like you and me."

"It seems at least you two are in a good starting position to move forward. Am I right?"

"I don't think so."

"That is a shame. If you were to engage, the Tikvah House for Young Jews would pay for your marriage ceremony."

"Whoa, that is far more than I expect to achieve with a girl I have just met."

"You *frei* are used to living meaningless lives."

"*Frei*?"

"*Frei*, it is Yiddish. It means 'free'; we use it with Jews like you, who are 'free' of observing the six hundred and thirteen precepts or *mitzvot* every Jew must observe."

"Six hundred thirteen. That is a lot of precepts."

"You see? I am right. You live meaningless lives."

"Well, I beg to disagree."

"And that is fine."

"You say we live meaningless lives but aren't your lives boring trying to observe all those rules?"

"Indeed, that is why we reach for fun trying to convince the *frei* to join us and make their lives holier."

Matt drank the last drops of beer, still sitting in his plastic glass.

"Well, that will not work with me."

"*A ber lernt men oykh oys tantsn,*" answered Shayna, smiling.

"And what does that mean?"

"It is a Yiddish proverb. It means that you can even teach a bear to dance with time. Think about it."

"I will," he said.

"So, if you don't devote your life to studying the Torah, what do you do?"

"I am a kind of journalist. I do some freelance projects here and there. I have a degree in English."

"Our sages say that a man should not write unless it is to honor *HaShem.*"

"Well, I don't know how honored *HaShem* is with the things I write, but at the very least, I hope I am not offending him."

"You are definitely offending him."

"And why is that?" said Matt, feeling slightly uneven.

"Our sages say that writing should be done only to honor *HaShem*. Men should only write to copy the scrolls of the Torah, not to write some news pieces in filthy magazines."

"That is incredibly offensive, you know?"

"What? I am just telling you how it is. With time…"

"… you can even teach a bear to dance. I get it. I find it rude that you call the magazines where my work is published filthy."

"I know enough to teach you what our sages preach. Please don't take the blame on me. I am just a messenger."

The loudspeakers stopped the music, and the voice of Rabbi Lehrer took its place. In a calm voice, he asked all his helpers to come down the street, where the Esther scroll would be read to the public.

"Let's go," said Shayna.

"Do we need to go? It sounds very boring."

"Come on. Give it a chance."

Matt accepted and followed Shayna and many others out of the Tikvah House and into the street, which was unusually busy and tumultuous. A scenario was mounted in the middle of the road, covered by red clothing with a Star of David in its center and *Mashiach* written below it.

"What is all that about the Messiah?" asked Matt.

"It is for all of us to remember that the true Messiah is coming soon," explained Shayna.

"How soon?"

"Don't worry. It is coming. We are going to see it during our lifetime. It could be tomorrow or maybe now. Why not?"

Matt thought that was insane, but he didn't share his thoughts with Shayna.

Two guys wearing SS uniforms passed by them.

"I know what you are thinking," said Shayna before he could articulate a word. "I don't like that kind of thing either. But don't worry; they are from Tikvah. They are just using a costume."

"But why?"

"While the official position Tikvah holds publicly supports the State of Israel, our sages oppose its existence. It is not us who will build our home state but the Messiah who will rebuild the Temple and bring all the Jews back to Jerusalem. Until he arrives, we cannot accept the current secular State of Israel."

"That is... ok, I guess. But it does not explain why the Nazi costumes."

"I haven't finished yet," Shayna grumbled, "some of our people believe that dressing up as the people who tried to exterminate us physically is preferable to dressing up as some Israeli soldier who represents the people trying to exterminate our souls."

"You realize what you have just told me makes little sense, right?"

"What can I say? Politics is everywhere, even within Tikvah. Also, it is Purim. So almost anything is permitted today."

"That means that this *frei* can kiss you, for example?"

Shayna blushed.

"No way," she said energetically, "that is not allowed at all. A *frei* must be with another *frei*. I am *frum*. I must be with another *frum*. Also, I am engaged."

"I didn't know."

"You might want to rejoin the other girl you passionately kissed before."

"Yeah," said Matt. Why had he tried that move? He wasn't sure. Shayna was a beautiful woman that was for sure, but it was something else that intrigued him about her. Maybe it was the fact that she was being so open about how Tikvah worked, telling him everything he needed to complete his report. "Never mind," he thought.

"Let's try to get closer to the scenario," said Shayna.

They went through the crowd.

"It seems like the stage is hollow, doesn't it?" said Matt.

"What do you mean?"

"Just that. It doesn't look exactly like a stage where someone will perform, but a hollow structure wrapped in cloth."

He had just finished pronouncing those words when the fabric came down like in a magician's trick. Matt was right. There wasn't a platform for performing or anything like that under it. Instead, there was a wooden altar. Laid on it was the pale bodies of two women with closed eyes; blood dripped from their slashed arms into a ceramic bowl in the ground. To its side, also written in blood, someone had written:

Pesach is approaching, and we must bake the matzah.

INTERLUDE

Malka threw a log into the fire. The heat was slowly waning. Outside, the road down to the banks of the Teteriv River was covered with a thick layer of snow. It seemed like time had stopped inside the run-down family home.

Isaac spent his days and nights reading the Torah scrolls, while Malka cared for their five children and ensured they always had something to eat, even when times were hard. They were having some stewed *bulbes* that day. It had been the same for the last few weeks. The children used to sing: "Sunday we have bulbes, Monday we have bulbes; Tuesday and Wednesday, bulbes; *Shabbos, tenks Got*, we have bulbe *kugel*, Sunday it's back to bulbes." And they were right. It was potato every single day.

The children had to spend all the time inside the house. Sometimes, they helped their mother, and during their free time, they played with a simple whirligig carved from a piece of wood. Malka thought that if the weather kept getting worse, even that would have to end in a fire. A great storm had stomped some trees nearby, but it was too dangerous for the children to go outside and grab them for the fire. Malka wasn't strong enough to do the heavy work either, and, of course, Isaac had to be inside reading the Torah. Josef, the oldest sibling, had gone outside a week ago and brought some lumber from the fallen trees, but nearly enough to pass the winter. As punishment for going outside, his father had prescribed he to read the Torah along with him. The child mainly complied. It had been from a piece of wood that he had brought that he had carved the whirligig that kept his younger siblings distracted most of the day.

It was sometime during the afternoon of that grey, dull day that someone knocked on their door. During that time of the year, it was not usual for people to go outside and meet others, so it took them by surprise. Isaac grunted some mean words to his wife, and she took off from the warm seat covered with deerskin to open the front door. A cold, cruel wind entered the house, almost killing the fire. The figure of a thin, tall man suddenly materialized. Malka recognized him immediately. It was the local rabbi, Jacob Aharonovich. He used to go by their house to discuss the Talmud while sharing some glasses of vodka with Isaac when the climate was more benign.

Malka was surprised to see him there.

"Rabbi, we weren't expecting you today with this snowstorm."

"Let me in, woman," said the rabbi violently while entering the house. "Where is the man of this house?" he shouted.

Isaac peered out from the house's only other room, where he and his wife slept and where he studied during the day.

"Malka, serve the rabbi a glass of vodka!" he cried. "Thank you, rabbi, for honoring my family and me with your presence during this fateful afternoon."

"Fateful are the times coming. I am afraid to tell," said the rabbi, shaking the snow from his boots. He took the glass of vodka Malka was now offering and swallowed it entirely.

"What is in your mind, rabbi?" asked Isaac.

The children continued playing with the whirligig as if nothing was happening.

"I came all the way from the synagogue to warn you of impending danger. Around an hour ago, I was studying the Torah when I was distracted by the sound of broken wood from the synagogue entrance. So I went to see what was happening and saw that someone had painted the door and that a crowd was gathering in front of the market square."

The face of Isaac turned sour and full of terror.

"I must warn as many good Jews as I can. A new *pogrom* is about to break at any moment."

Malka, who had been hearing everything from the side, went to their children and reunited them in a big hug.

"There has been a new blood libel. The baker's daughter, a Christian girl, has been found dead in the forest. People in the market chanted that the Jews killed her so we could use her blood for kneading *matzah*."

"That is nonsense!" screamed Isaac.

"But they believe it, and that is enough for them to want to kill us all," said the rabbi resigned.

"What is your suggestion, rabbi?"

"Pack your things and get out. As soon and as far as possible."

"But there is a snowstorm happening right now!" said Malka.

"Shut up, woman! Haven't you heard our guest? Do you want to get killed by a mob of angry Christians?"

Malka didn't answer her husband. Instead, she told her children to grab something to cover themselves and prepare to go outside.

They grabbed what they could and went outside the house with the rabbi. Malka carried a pot of bulbe to feed themselves that night; Isaac held a *sefer* Torah next to his chest, and Josef carried the whirligig he had carved for his siblings. The rabbi led the way as they left their little belongings. Then, some angry, loud voices reached them. The fire from burning torches started to pour from the forest trees surrounding them.

"To the river!" screamed Isaac to his family.

They tried to change their path, but it was already too late. The torches were almost over them.

"Assassins of Christ! Murderers!" the screaming mob was over them.

"Heretics!"

"You murdered little Halina Brunnow!"

"Filthy animals! You will not get away with this murder!"

The mob surrounded the family, and Isaac tried to explain in Yiddish that they had nothing to do with the death of the baker's daughter.

"Shut your filthy mouths!" said a man who seemed to be the mob's leader. "We are aware of how you Jews use the blood of Christian children for baking your bread!"

"That is a lie! An absolute lie!" said the rabbi, blushing in ire.

"We have killed no one," said Malka, crying.

"It is time that you Jews pay for all the damage you have done to our community," said another man emerging from the mob.

"We have nothing to do with your suffering," said Isaac to the mob, speaking in poor Polish.

"The Jews are the ones that crush us by collecting taxes for the nobility!" said a furious farmer.

"He speaks the truth!" agreed another one.

The rabbi interposed his body again between the terrified family and the angry mob.

"Let these people go. They have children. They have done nothing to the Christians. I will answer in trial for the accusations against these poor people and all the Jews in Zhytomyr."

Some loud murmurs came from the mob. Big, round, and heavy snowflakes continued to fall. The farmer that had spoken before angrily exclaimed, "Let's not fall into their traps again! Let's kill them right here and right now!"

Screams of approbation followed him. Then, saying nothing else, the farmer stroked his fork into the rabbi's chest, breaking through his heart. A spade struck Isaac in the face as he was falling to the ground. Malka threw herself onto the ground, trying to comfort her husband, who was already dead. A sickle cut her throat, and her body fell over his. The children were hanged from the prominent branch of a centennial oak. A few hours later, the only remaining massacre was the red-colored snow and the abandoned whirligig below the hanged corpses of the children that swayed ten feet above the ground.

Josef, the oldest sibling, was still hiding behind some bushes. He had slipped away while the mob was still deliberating and had temporarily saved his life. He looked at his dead siblings and parents, who were already becoming hidden under the snow that hadn't ceased to fall. He then ran into the forest without looking back.

Chapter 14

Matt

It wasn't until noon the following day that Matt could finally return to his apartment. With so many witnesses, it had taken that long until he could tell the police what he had seen. It was much the same as what the other hundreds of witnesses had: nothing. Just the dead bodies of the two women at the altar and their slashed arms bleeding into a stone bowl. After he was let go, he took a taxi directly to the apartment; he disconnected his phone and went straight to bed. He slept for nine hours of uninterrupted nightmares. He woke up feeling wasted.

"What now?" he asked himself while trying to understand what had happened the day before. The whole situation just felt unreal. The costumes, the party, the sweating, the kiss with Denise, the conversation with the ginger girl, and finally, the horror of the bloody corpses on display so everyone could see them. After the theatrical apparition of the bodies, all chaos broke loose. Not immediately, as many thought that was part of the show, like a magician's trick or something like that. It was Purim, after all, and as Shayna had told him, almost everything was allowed during the festivity. But then someone got involved and started shouting that the women were really dead, that it wasn't a joke, and that they weren't just dummies but real women that had been killed. Then, it all went sour. People started screaming and running, and many got into each other. Some people were even hurt. Matt hadn't been able to get in touch with Shayna after all the confusion, but he did spot her at the police station. She seemed to repeat something to herself, but he couldn't quite hear it. Judging by her lips' movement, he guessed she was repeating something about "blood veils." It made little sense to him, but almost nothing related to Tikvah and the Hasidim made sense now for him. It was like going back to square one. After waiting a while at the police station, he saw a big man looking like a sage entering and going directly to talk with Shayna. He had then talked with a police officer, and Shayna had left with him. Matt, instead, had to wait much longer before being asked what had happened the night before and then let go.

What would he do now? First, he needed to speak with Margaret Wainstein and ask her how to continue. Things had changed radically. But first, he knew he had to talk with his mother. So he re-connected his phone and called her. His mother had seen everything on the TV but seemed unaware he had been there.

"Again, these people. The ones that took poor David."

"Yes. I know, Mum."

He would not tell her about his involvement, and he would call his brother as soon as he hung out with her so that he wouldn't tell her either. He then received a call from Margaret Wainstein.

"Hello. I was thinking of calling you." He said.

"Listen to me, Matthew," said the woman directly, "this is becoming much darker than I expected. I will send Carlos Ortega to continue this investigation. You are relieved from duty. Take the money and forget about this entire thing."

"Well, I was just trying to tell you I have a preliminary report."

"That is fine. Send whatever you have compiled and leave it there. Carlos will take the lead now. I know what you are thinking. Why didn't I send him in the first place? I didn't expect that there would be more bodies in the way. And Carlos... is a much tougher guy than you are. No offense. He has seen and done a lot of things in his life."

"No offense taken. I remember he told me something about having been a police officer in Mexico," mumbled Matt, who had been taken by surprise by this new development.

"You have no idea, Matt. But it is fine. Let's leave it like that. Send me the report and forget about the matter," said the woman, hanging up without saying goodbye.

Well, that was it. He returned the telephone to his desk and returned to the computer screen. "Blood veils" he searched in Google but only found information regarding a video game. Nothing he could see Shayna caring about.

He then tried to read the news but grew disgusted almost immediately. According to the police, Rabbi Abraham Lehrer was a person of interest in the case and was being intensely searched for. Nobody noticed when he vanished from the party. There also had been anti-Semitic attacks in the city since last night, mainly targeted against Hasidim. He felt disgusted. Also, he felt like he could not just let everything go. He needed to speak with someone. He decided to visit the Marshall Blum Center. It was a social and sports club for secular-minded Jews like himself. He had worked half-time in the club's library during his college years for about three years. Nevertheless, he never really got into the Jewish life aspects of the center. It was just a place where he could make some money by recommending books to the club members and maybe help a researcher or two looking for some rare book they held in the library.

Also, he was granted access to the gym and swimming pool as an employee, so it was worth it. But now, he felt like he could talk with Debra, the senior librarian who had been her boss during his time working there. She might hold some clue about what was happening.

The first thing that caught his eye when he arrived was how the security measures had changed since his time. A security guard interrogated him before letting him enter. That he had worked there did not impress the man, who only let him in after calling Debra and asking her if she was okay with letting him in. Once inside, he had to undergo another security check before finally reaching the library.

He saw Debra standing behind the desk he used when working there and suddenly felt like a tornado of memories of good times had touched him.

"Good to see you, Matt. What brings you here after all this time?" saluted him, his former boss. It was as if time had not passed for her and the library, which looked exactly like the last day he had seen it. Some new books were on display, but the rest looked precisely the same. Tons of books in precise order resting on the Victorian mahogany bookshelves. It was still early in the day, so there weren't many people studying or reading at the tables, but he could recognize some faces from back in the day.

"Nice to see you too, Debra. What brings me here is the strange times we are living."

Her face seemed to lose its joy.

"What do you mean, exactly?"

"This," said Matt, pointing to the news piece on the paper Debra was reading. "I was there when all that happened." He said.

"I am so sorry."

"Thank you. Anyway, I thought that maybe you could help me."

"What could I possibly help you with?"

"Maybe to understand."

"Come on, Matt!" she said, losing her posture. "There is nothing I could tell you about this! You were the one who was there!"

"I know, but I must insist."

"You want my advice? Leave it as it is and carry on with your life. I am sorry you had this experience. Now move over."

"It is too late for that."

"What do you mean?"

"Remember my friend David? I told you about him. About how we were together in a car accident, how when he was recovering from the injuries, he started to surround himself with some orthodox Jews, and shortly after, he ended up joining them."

"Yes, I remember," said Debra.

"You know what happened to him and his family a few weeks ago, right? It was all over the news."

"Of course, I know what happened. And that is why I am telling you to let all this go. This is not something you fool around."

"I am aware. I only need a straightforward favor from you."

"And what would that be?"

"I just need if you could tell me where can I find information about something called 'blood veils.' It is something that might be related to this whole situation."

Debra thought for a moment.

"I don't think there is such a thing. Not at least that I have heard."

"Nothing? Nothing in the Jewish history and tradition?"

"No. I am sorry. Where did you come up with that?"

"I heard someone repeating to herself those words in shock. It was after discovering the two bodies of those poor women."

Debra was still thinking, trying to come up with something.

"Are you sure it is 'blood veils' that you are looking for? Because I assure you will not find any subject with that name in this library."

"I see," said Matt, disappointed. So that was that. He would probably have to give up on the case after all.

"However," said Debra, "you might find something about 'blood libels' if that interests you."

"What would that be?"

"Well, you can just look at the newspaper and see how they start. All these false accusations against us, Jews, are the root of all anti-Semitism. The lies about how we supposedly kill Christians and all that."

"You know what? Maybe you are right, and I got the name of what I am looking for wrong."

"In that case, I can help you. Give me some days to look at blood libels in our catalog, and I will call you back. But please, be careful."

Matt thanked Debra and got out to the street. His mobile phone rang. The screen read: "Mike."

He picked up the call and said, "I was just thinking about talking to you."

CHAPTER 15

ORTEGA

C arlos Ortega took another look at the pile of papers on his desk. He made himself comfortable in the seat, took a cigarette out of his shirt pocket, and held it on his fingers for a few seconds before taking it to his mouth. He lit it and took the smoke into his lungs as long as possible before letting it out. It had been easy for him to get the forensic report. He had some friends, and the open wallet of Ms. Wainstein's had done the rest. The names of the victims said little: Juana Rocío García and Marisa Milagros García, mother and daughter from where he had also come many years ago. It was the same road of tears, with different endings so far.

The report said they had died of bleeding and had been drugged with sleeping pills hours before their corpses were found. Both women had worked for Tikvah House for Young Jews for years until that night. The suspect, Rabbi Abraham Lehrer, was being intensively searched for by the police. Still, it didn't seem like they would make a breakthrough soon. Ortega suspected someone in an influential position was lending the man a helpful hand. The whole thing seemed too elaborate and complicated for just one person to perform and escape without a trace. What bothered him was that there were no witnesses. Plenty of witnesses had seen when the corpses had been theatrically revealed; still, no one seemed to have seen when that altar had been put, when the women had been killed, or where. It was almost as if the two women had voluntarily climbed the altar, lay there, voluntarily taken the pills, and waited for a butcher to cut their wrists. They had no family living in the country, and the police had only contacted a distant relative living in Monterrey who had declined to take the trip north to recognize the bodies. They were, therefore, headed for the mass grave.

Ortega had visited the rooming house where the women had lived for the previous years that morning to learn more. It was a tidy, decent room in a dilapidated structure. A Latina woman in her late sixties was in charge, and it had been easy for Ortega to make her talk.

"They were good *gente*," said the woman, sweeping the entrance. "It is a shame what happened to them."

"Can you tell me anything else about them?"

"I've already told everything I know to the police. They were good people. They always paid their rent on time. They didn't go out much, and they lived together."

"When was the last time you saw them alive?"

The woman gave it a long thought.

"I cannot say. It might have been months ago. I barely saw them as they were mostly inside their room, and they only went out during the night when I am usually sleeping."

"Did they pay their rent on time?"

"Always. They would slip an envelope with cash under my door."

"Do you recall them having any kind of trouble with other of your tenants?"

"Nothing. Never. They were *santas*. I truly am sorry about what happened to them."

"I see," said Ortega, a little perplexed. He asked the woman for a list of the other tenants. While the woman initially resisted, he convinced her with a hundred bill. It had been in vain either way, as the people he could question had nothing to add to what the woman had told him.

And now he was alone with his thoughts and the papers on his desk, trying to make sense of all that. But it was not working. He had to admit that the crime seemed to lead to a dead end. At least until they apprehended Rabbi Abraham Leherer. That was what bothered him the most. With such a spectacular display, it had to be more open. There needed to be some loose end, but he couldn't see it yet. Why mount such a spectacle?

According to the testimonies, Rabbi Abraham Lehrer was a fervent, committed man of faith who had devoted his entire adult life to working for the success of his community. Nobody could believe that he could have turned into a killer. What for? Why destroy all his life's work? There were no answers, and that was all that he had. Empty hands and running empty of ideas about how to move forward.

He looked at his small black leather notepad. It had been with him since he had been promoted to Murder Detective. Even though it was falling apart and had almost no blank spots left, he considered it a talisman. Ortega knew it was a silly idea, but he had made it alive out of Mexico, hadn't he? Yes, he had left a woman and a daughter there, and he would probably never see them again. It was a price he had to pay to stay alive. He was used to sacrifices, but this other sacrifice, this human sacrifice, he couldn't understand it. He witnessed many atrocities during his time, including decapitating men and acid-burning bodies. Still, those were justified in the circumstances. These poor women with their wrists sliced that was simply absurd.

He tapped the cover of the black leather notepad with the tip of his fingers and opened it again. He went over his markings for the case and was just about to put it back on the table when he noticed a name he had scribbled at the end of one page. He hadn't noticed it before and couldn't remember when he had written it. It said "Melanie Sirota," and he had written a telephone number on its side.

Who could she be? He didn't remember writing that name. But he had. His only clues were that name and a report about the killing weapon, a butcher's knife. The knife had animal blood stains besides human blood.

He got up from the seat, took a last puff of the cigarette in his lips, and then threw it into the trash bin beside the desk. He thought he was getting an idea but still didn't fully understand it. He went back to the seat and closed his eyes for a moment. He then put his crossed legs on the table and fell asleep for a few minutes. It was a short but intense dream. He saw the killing victims standing with their wrists open and bleeding. They were already dead and rotten. He then woke up, startled.

"Time to go back to work," he thought while reaching for the phone on the desk. He tipped the number of Melanie Sirota. It took three rings until a timid woman's voice said "Hello" on the other side of the line.

CHAPTER 16

SHAYNA

For all she knew, it was happening all over again. Her father had begun the process of forgetting another family member. This time, it was her uncle Abraham. His father had stopped mentioning him since he had vanished following the murder of the cook and her daughter at his Tikvah House. Even though he hadn't been officially excommunicated from the community, his name was prohibited in his house or elsewhere in Tikvah Zhytomyr. *Yimakh shemo ve zikhro*, may his name and his memory be erased. The same thing that had happened ten years ago with her sister was now happening again with her uncle. Shayna desperately wanted to ask his father what was going on. Still, because she was a woman, she had to keep quiet. These were men's problems; they would not share them with her or any other women.

The week following the Purim killings, during the Hasidic reunion during Shabbos in his synagogue, Rabbi Moshe Lehrer pronounced sobering words that deepened the necessity for the community to follow the path of the Torah and don't let be fooled by false idols. He had told them, with a tight face that was trying hard not to cry, that no Tikvah Hasid should get confused and let dangerous ideas that would tear the community apart take root in their minds. And as soon as he had said that, he punched the table and almost yelled that from then on, there would be no tolerance for any internal disagreement or talking about what had just happened. No one should talk about those things, not between community members, much less with the Gentiles. Anyone who dared to do it anyway would be expelled from the community without appeal.

Shayna and the other women in the synagogue heard what her father said from the balcony on the second floor, away from the men. After he pronounced those words, all the men started chanting some sweet Hasidic songs. Shortly after, most of them also got completely drunk. She had correctly foreseen that would happen, so she had planned to escape his father's fierce control during that time. She was to meet Matt at the bar where she was when her sister was killed. Shayna knew it would be a risky move, but she needed to try it anyway.

Things were getting worse, not only inside Tikvah's community but elsewhere. There had been some reported attacks on Hasidim and Jews from other communities and even secular Jews. Shayna only heard about those incidents by gossip, as always. The kinds of things women would tell her mother: "Do you remember Mendel, the son of Dina and Pinjas Grimberg? He was beaten on his way to the Yeshiva the other day," or "Have you seen? David, the son of Yehuda and Miriam Kuravsky, was intercepted the other day in the street. They told him racial slurs and accused him of being a murderer."

She entered the bar feeling more confident than the last time. She was still wearing her Shabbos' traditional clothes, which weren't that much different from the ones she used to wear daily. However, they still got the attention of patrons who weren't used to seeing that kind of prude woman in the bar. To her relief, Matt was already there when she got inside. He sat alone at a table away from the others. Shayna approached him directly. She sat down in front of him.

"Thank you for coming to meet me," she said. "This feels weird for me."

He looked at her with compassion.

"Are you having something to drink?"

"I think I am fine for now."

"Does it bother you?" he said, pointing to a glass of whisky on the table.

"It will be fine if you don't lose your composure."

"Great," he said, taking a sip from his glass, "so, the last thing I remember is you were telling me you are engaged."

Shayna certainly hadn't expected the conversation to start like that. She blushed.

"That is correct. It was arranged by my father and my fiancée's father. I barely know him."

"And are you comfortable with things going like that?"

"Well, it is how we do things in Tikvah; so comfortable or uncomfortable, it doesn't matter as it won't change anything."

Matt seemed impressed.

"I don't understand why you agreed to this."

"Why not? Don't you do things you dislike or care about because you must?"

"All the time. But not in things like getting married. You will have to share your life with someone you don't love."

"I don't love him now. Why can't I learn to love him later? Ultimately, love is nothing more than getting used to someone to the point that you care. Isn't it?"

"I don't think so. And I feel sorry that you think that."

"Well, you can feel whatever you want, but discussing my marriage is not why I set this meeting."

"You are right. Why did you call me, then?"

"I called you because you were beside me the day of the murders. You saw what I saw and maybe something more. I need to know what happened. I need all this madness to stop."

"And why did you think of me? Police investigators are in charge."

"I know how the police and the entire justice system like Jews. So, I don't trust them."

"Fair enough, but once again, I must ask you, why me?"

"It may sound a little odd to you, but the fact is that you are the only *frei* I know and have talked more than a few words. I need to talk with someone outside Tikvah to help me untangle all this."

Matt started feeling paranoid, as if she knew he had been reading up on them before the recent murders.

"All this is... fine, I guess. But I don't know how I can assist you with your criminal investigation or whatever you want to call it. And also, what would be in for me?"

Shayna smiled. She had been expecting that moment.

"You also have good reasons to try to end this mystery, don't you?"

Matt attempted to play the fool.

"I don't know what you are talking about."

"About a month ago, two other Tikvah Hasidim committed suicide and murdered their children in a manner strikingly similar to what we saw the other day. We hadn't talked in years, but that woman was my sister. And you were connected to them in some way as well."

Matt froze. Trying to maintain a very calm tone of voice, he asked her,

"How do you know about my relationship with David?"

"I only know that you knew him."

"It was more than that. He and I were best friends as children until our first youth."

"Then I was right. You were related to him."

"Now it is your turn to tell me how you know."

"It was easy. What do you think we do with the information we collect from people who start attending our activities?"

Matt felt a shudder through his spine.

"So, you spy on everyone who goes for free sushi on a Saturday night at a Tikvah House?"

"Well, people not only come for the free sushi."

"You are right, also the trips to Israel, the matchmaking, all those things."

"There is much more you could get. And all for free."

"I think I will pass. I want to keep my privacy from now on."

"Says the guy who has given all his personal information to big tech companies."

"You seem to know much about the modern world for being part of a conservative religious sect."

"Technology is also a gift from HaShem."

Matt took another sip from his glass of whisky.

"Well, I am kind of impressed," he said.

"And also a little wasted."

"That is not the point."

"There is something more."

"You tell me. But I doubt you will surprise me anymore."

"Do you want to bet on it?" she said, smiling.

"Isn't betting forbidden on your worldview? Whatever, bring it on."

"You seemed unsurprised when the two murdered women appeared the other day. Like if you were expecting it somehow."

Matt hadn't felt that way, but she could have a point. Maybe he was expecting something like that to happen after David's actions.

"Just for you to know, neither your friend nor my sister were good Hasidim or Jews. They had been expelled from Tikvah by my father. I guess my uncle isn't a good Jew as well. At some point, they missed the way. That is precisely what I want to understand and why I need help from someone who can see things from the outside."

"Even though I finally have a better idea of your intentions, I still don't get what you want from me."

"We could have a professional relationship if you like. Not that I could pay you, but don't you write for a living? You could make a good news piece out of all this."

"I must admit, it seems interesting."

"Great, then we will be in touch. Now I need to get home."

"Already?" said Matt, looking at his watch. "It is still early!"

"Every second it passes, the stakes of being discovered profaning Shabbos grow."

"I understand. But before you leave, what do you know about 'blood libels'?"

Shayna wasn't expecting that.

"Where did you hear those words?"

"You were repeating them to yourself the day after the Purim incident."

"It is just something my uncle said to me before the murders. I know nothing apart from that they exist."

"Well, I already did some research. They were non-factual accusations against Jews made by Christians during the Middle Ages. They basically accused Jews of sacrificing Christian children in black magic rituals."

"Just like what we saw the other day."

"Exactly. Except that this time it was real."

"Why? Why did it happen?"

"Well, I think that is what we have to unravel, right?"

Shayna felt a little stunned.

"Let's think about this and talk in the coming days. Wait for my call."

Matt stayed in his seat while she took off and walked toward the exit.

Upon reaching the street, Shayna took a big breath. She was feeling dizzy and confused and just wanted to get home. She walked a few steps when she felt a shadow following her. She walked faster, but then the shadow stretched and grabbed her arm. She stopped, terrified.

"Shabbat Shalom, Shayna Lehrer. I see you have opted to desecrate Shabbos again," said a voice behind her.

CHAPTER 17

ORTEGA

"Am I talking with Melanie Sirota?"

"Who is this?"

"Carlos Ortega, P.I."

There was a silence on the other side of the line, only interrupted by heavy breathing. He finally heard the woman swallowing saliva and say,

"I don't want to talk anymore or to anyone else. I have already said what I know to the police."

"We both know that the police are letting this case go cold. Do you want to live the rest of your life fearing the assassin reaching you?"

He now heard some sobbing.

"Please, don't do this to me. I just want it to be over."

"My client also wants this to be over. If you cooperate, I assure you I will do my best so that becomes a reality, and you won't have to worry about being chased by a psycho anymore."

"Fine. What do you want from me, then?"

"Just to ask you a few questions."

"Go ahead."

"I was thinking of meeting in person. Would you be okay with that?"

Forty minutes later, Ortega rang the bell in a modest suburban house. It was a cold, humid day, and Ortega was filling aches in his bones. The door opened, and he felt warmth from the heating system through his face. A tall, thin man around his age stood beside the opened door.

"You must be Ortega."

"Yes, sir."

"Come in, please. I am Augustus Sirota, Melanie's father. I hope you don't mind if I stay while you speak to my daughter."

"No objection."

"Fine. Please follow me, then."

Ortega followed the man to an open living room with mushy caramel-colored carpet and a set of sofas in the same color. The walls were decorated with abstract paintings; in the corners were ceramic vases on marble columns. Ortega knew little art or decoration but could tell it was in poor taste.

Melanie was sitting on the sofa. She looked pale and had bags under her eyes, as if she hadn't slept well for weeks. Her hair was messy, and a nervous tic in her left eyebrow prompted it to move out of her control.

The girl's father offered Ortega a chair to sit on before Melanie. He took off his black notepad and sat.

"Good day, Melanie. I am Carlos Ortega. As I told you over the phone, I am a private investigator. My client is as interested as yourself in uncovering the truth behind the awful murder you witnessed."

The girl nodded affirmatively.

"Do you have questions before we start?"

"No, no, let's just get over this."

"Great. Let's begin with some basic fact-checking. I understand you worked for the Tikvah House for Young Jews until the recent murders. Is that correct?"

"That is correct."

"Since when you started working there?"

"She was a volunteer, not a worker," intervened her father, sitting beside her.

"Please, let Melanie answer the questions," said Ortega, irritated.

"My father is right. I volunteered for almost a year."

"And what brought you to volunteer there?"

"Well," she said and took a moment to think what she wanted to say, "here in this family, we are Jews who have been unaware of the truth for most of our lives. So, when we finally found it, I realized I had to do something for our community. I asked around a little about the possibility of working at the Tikvah House for Young Jews, and I took it. Simply as that."

"What do you mean when you say that you found the truth? Who found it? What truth?"

"What my daughter is saying is that we raised her as a secular Jew, as we also were. Then, a few years ago, we found the teachings of Tikvah's rebbe and became aware of the authentic ways for the Jews," said Augustus.

"You mean you became religious?"

"Observant is our preferred term."

"Right," said Ortega while taking note. "When you volunteered at Tikvah's youth center, did you notice something strange about the head rabbi?"

"Nothing at all," said Melanie with confidence.

"And what type of activities did you perform as a volunteer?"

"Mostly paperwork, secretary to Rabbi Lehrer, and helped welcome people during festivals and events."

"So, you were secretary to the rabbi."

"That is what I said."

"You managed his agenda?"

"Among other things, yes."

"Do you still have, by any chance, access to that agenda?"

"I keep a backup copy on my Google Calendar."

"Would you mind if I look at it?"

She extracted her cell phone from the pocket of his pants. After a few touches, she had Abraham Lehrer's agenda opened.

"Here, look whatever you want," she said, handing him her phone.

He took a detailed look at the calendar. There were meetings with people he could recognize because they were public figures. Millionaires, Hollywood producers, and businessmen. He had even met some of them in person, as Margaret Wainstein's law firm had represented them. To the side of most of the names, he saw the annotation "donor."

"So, these donors donated to the youth center?"

"Exactly."

"How impressive."

"Rabbi Lehrer knows how to open wallets."

"Well, at least until the murders, I suppose," reflected Ortega and was received by icy silence.

He looked at the rest of the meetings.

"Here it says that a few weeks ago, Rabbi Lehrer had two meetings with another rabbi, Isaac Setzer?"

"That is correct."

"Were the meetings between the two common?"

"Sometimes. Rabbi Abraham would usually meet with his brothers or with any other volunteers. He is... or maybe was, I don't know now, a truly busy man."

"What can you tell me about this, Rabbi Isaac?"

"Not much. I know he runs his center in El Paso, Texas, and that he and Rabbi Abraham had those meetings during the last weeks. It may be related to the recent conference that rabbi Isaac gave at the youth center."

"I see," said Ortega while reading the date on the calendar of the recent conference by Rabbi Setzer. "Do you know if the two were friends besides their professional relationship?"

"It is hard to tell. Rabbi Abraham is a people person. He seemed to get along with everybody. He and Rabbi Isaac seemed to be close, though."

Ortega took further notes.

"A last question, Melanie. Why weren't you at the youth center the night of the crime?"

A small tear dropped on her cheek.

"Rabbi Abraham forbade me to attend. I was prohibited from going the entire week leading up to that evening. He said I had violated some precepts and had to learn my lesson. I couldn't tell which precepts I disrespected, and he would not tell me upon asking him."

"How convenient."

"Are you accusing my daughter?" asked Augustus Sirota, playing defense.

"Absolutely not. Despite everything Abraham Lehrer did, he seemed to hold a soft spot in his heart for Melanie. He made up a pretext to keep her away while he plotted and executed his crime."

"Those women," said Melanie, "they were simple people. Yes, they were goyim, but they didn't deserve that horrible thing that happened to them."

"Did you know them?"

"I saw the two of them a few times while volunteering at the center. Never spoke to them more than the strictly necessary, but that doesn't mean I don't feel sorry for them."

Ortega closed his notepad and took off from the chair.

"Thank you for your collaboration," he said. Augustus Sirota escorted him back to the street.

Chapter 18

Shayna

"I see you have opted to desecrate Shabbos once again," repeated a distorted voice before she could turn around and confront the man behind her.

"Let's continue walking," said her fiancée, rabbi Mordechai Posner.

Shayna didn't say a word and kept walking with him.

"It happened right before a night of Shabbos in five thousand five hundred ninety-nine, or if you prefer, one thousand eight hundred and thirty-nine," said Mendel Posner, "Rabbi Menachem Mendel of Kotzk, the first Rebbe of Kotzk, was preparing for the night when suddenly, something happened. It was freezing outside, and the cold poured through the miserable houses of our cousins in Poland. But nobody felt the pain of that cold because it was Shabbos, and everybody was full of joy, waiting for the rabbi to bless the wine and bread. But the rabbi, instead, just became immobile as if he had become frozen. His eyes went blank, but the surrounding people could tell he was still there. It was like he was in a kind of silent meditation. Everyone went silent. The oil lamps illuminated a scene that was of absolute immobility. Outside, terrible winds were blowing. Its whirring was the only thing that could be heard. Then, the rabbi moved his head backward and stood in that position for a good time."

Shayna was attentively following the narrative and attempting to decipher its moral. She had always heard with meaningful joy the moralizing stories that the Hasidim had for every occasion in life. But, now that she had been found breaking the sacredness of Shabbat, she was sure that the conclusion had to be a veiled warning. However, she couldn't completely grasp it from what Mordechai had told her.

"The story doesn't end here," said Mordechai, breaking the menacing atmosphere he had created. "After a while, the rabbi woke up, got up from his chair, went to the lit candles, and blew them out one by one, effectively profaning Shabbos. Then, as suddenly as he had gone into a trance, he fainted. His Hasidim took him to his bed, and while he regained consciousness a few hours later, he stayed in his bedroom for over twenty years. Nothing no one ever said to him during that time could convince him to leave the bedroom. He just got used to living there, where he spent most of his time reading the Torah, and his Hasidim did everything they could to accommodate him. No one would ever try to contradict him, of course."

Shayna was still struggling to understand what her fiancée was trying to tell her, and maybe because he perceived her confusion, he added,

"I will not tolerate your unholy behavior anymore, Shayna Lehrer. Your father is very concerned about you, especially considering what is happening now in our community. I am sure he wouldn't take it with grace if our marriage were to be canceled."

"I understand," she murmured.

"Good. For this same reason, I arranged for our wedding to be held before the initial date we discussed. I want us to be married so we can move to Jerusalem as soon as possible."

Those last words fell over Shayna as if she were being buried alive. A wave of heat moved around her body, giving her the certainty that she could not stand that anymore. She could not keep living and believing in anything Tikvah Zhytomyr stood for. She now realized she no longer cared about Hasidic tales, their festivities, and much less the man she was supposed to marry.

With a perfectly calm tone, she said to him,

"Rabbi Posner, don't take this personally, but I am not interested in your plans."

The man stopped on his feet.

"What are you insinuating?" he said, alarmed.

"I am not insinuating anything. I am telling you. But now that you brought that up, I will insinuate to see if you get it better this time. Rabbi Wolf from Zhytomyr once said: «I do not understand those people that pretend to be illuminated and are always seeking answers from faith. For us who have faith, there are no questions; for those who do not have faith, there are no answers.»"

"I am glad you know about this tzaddiq of ours," said Mordechai. "You may also know that on his deathbed, he famously said that he had seen in a vision that the world would lose stability and people would lose their senses. I think he was right, Shayna. You have clearly lost your mind. And it is a perilous path that you are walking. Especially during these strange days, we are going through."

"And what would happen to me?" asked Shayna, furious. "What is my father going to do? Will he expel me from the community as he did with my sister?"

The man took Shayna's arm and moved her towards him.

"Don't go searching for Succubus, Shayna. They are closer than you think." His eyes were blood red, and his tone was dead serious.

Shayna stood there without moving, expecting something more. Still, her fiancée just limited himself to looking at her with his ignited eyes for a few seconds that seemed to her like they would never end.

He then started walking, and she followed him. They did the rest of the way to her home in silence. When they arrived, he told her to remember what they had talked about that night and left.

Shayna went inside and saw the light coming from her father's studio. She knew he had been waiting for her. Her father was behind his desk reading the Talmud.

"Take a seat," he said without moving his eyes from the old, yellowish pages of the book he had opened before him.

She looked at his father. He seemed tired as if he had gotten twenty years older in just a few weeks. She sat in the chair in front of him.

"What you have done tonight, dear daughter, is a terrible sin, a betrayal of the laws that guide our people. And worst of all, it is not your first time doing something like this. You have been going against me, your family, your community, and all the Jewish people. You deserve nothing less than being expelled from Tikvah Zhytomyr. You have never heard me say what I am about to and won't hear me repeat it: I have already lost a daughter. That is the only reason you are still part of this community. But be aware that I will not tolerate any more of your miscarries," said the rabbi.

"Well, I find it very stimulating that you are finally willing to talk about Chaia. So I would like to talk about her a little more."

"Silence, child. Haven't you heard what I have just said?"

"Yes, and so is why I am taking the opportunity to talk about my sister with you."

"You have nothing to say, much less to ask. You are a woman. You are here to obey what the men of your community say to you. And I am your father, so you will listen carefully and shut up."

Shayna got up from the chair.

"Is there anything else you want to tell me? If not, I am eager to go to sleep."

"Sit down! You have disrespected your family and me enough! You have just confirmed that my plans for you are the only way this can move on. You will spend the few weeks until your wedding living in Tikvah Women's House. You will be under the strict care and supervision of Rachel Buman. You are to do whatever she commands you to do. You may not go out at any time of the day or night until your wedding. This is the only option you have left me. I expect you to know this has come because of your actions alone."

Shayna was feeling furious and impotent. She knew she could do nothing to escape the sentence his father had just given her.

"And I hope you understand this is the shortest way to lose your only remaining daughter."

"I told you to shut up! What has happened to you, Shayna? All the education and care I provided for you, all these years of love and community, for you to come to the office of the great Moshe Lehrer, *shaliah* of Tikvah's Rebbe, to make these ridiculous arguments? To desecrate Shabbos and insult me?" the rabbi shook uncontrollably. "You are going to the women's boarding school tonight and staying there until I decide! That's all there is to it." He then took his phone and said a few words in Yiddish. After that, a pair of Hasidic men entered the studio and positioned to the sides of Shayna.

"Now, go," he said

Shayna was silently sobbing. She was at a loss for what to do next.

The men told her to walk. They would do anything to avoid touching her arms, but Shayna knew they wouldn't hesitate to use their physical strength to get her back if she tried to run away. His father was taking her. The men conducted her all three deserted blocks to Tikvah Women's boarding school.

"Truth is the safest lie," the Yiddish proverb came to her mind. She wanted it to make sense in that context that someone explained what was happening. Still, everybody in the community seemed more comfortable living within lies.

The way to the boarding school felt like a death march. When they finally arrived, she looked at the impressive five-story building with mirrored windows. It looked like a luxury hotel. She was escorted inside, where Rachel Buman was waiting for her. Shayna could not believe that she would comply with his father's order. Rachel was someone she had known since birth. Rachel had raised her and held Shayna in her arms. And now, Rachel had accepted to become her prison guard.

"Welcome, dear," said the woman with a big, compassionate smile.

Shayna didn't answer.

"Let me show you your room. It is one of the best we have. Like a presidential suite."

Shayna followed her in silence to the room. Rachel wasn't lying. The room looked gorgeous and provided an impressive look to the cityscape. However, it was also very modest. It had a comfortable bed, a desk with a flower pot, some fresh Jasmine flowers, and a praying book. The unmissable portrait of Shmuel Abraham Josefson Bunem, Tivka's last Rebbe, hanged on the wall, with all his imposing seriousness.

"Now rest, Shayna. It is too late," said Rachel Buman. "Tomorrow, we will have a wonderful meeting with Rabbi Goldfarb. He is going to share some Hasidic tales. After that, we may sing a little. You will see. It is going to be a beautiful day tomorrow." After saying this, Rachel left the room, leaving Shayna alone.

She was in shock. Everything had happened so fast, and she was still trying to grasp her new reality. Just when she had started building her road, all this happened. She thought about Matt. That *frei*. He was free, in effect. He could go wherever he wanted and do whatever he felt like doing. He wasn't forced to get married to someone he didn't know. And he could start investigating what was behind the crimes as they had arranged.

At least the room was nice, she thought. The lights were warm and soft. The walls were covered in a wallpaper that resembled rose marble. She felt some peace being there, although she knew this was her prison cell. Nothing more, nothing less. She went to the table and grabbed the prayer book. She passed through the pages and questioned the act of praying for the first time in her life. What was the sense of doing that? Outside that ivory tower where she was being held prisoner, Jews and Gentiles were getting killed, and something or someone was driving people to commit craziness. And she had nowhere to go. Her father, family, and community had put rules over her head her entire life. There were guidelines for when to pray, how to sleep, what to read, what to study and what not to study, and even what to say when using the restroom. Soon, she would get married, and new rules would be imposed on her: how to care about her future husband, the obligation of having children, the tasks she would have to do in their future home, even when she would have intercourse with him. Just as important was when she would not even be able to sleep in the same bed as her husband. That would be when she had her period, and she would have to clean her impureness every month after that. She realized that her body had been controlled during her entire life. It would still be controlled and would even be controlled after her death when she would be buried following traditional Hasidic rules.

Shayna felt exhausted and lay down in bed again until she fell asleep.

She was woken up by Shterna Daye, Rachel's right hand. And it took Shayna little time to discover that she had been assigned to control her at every moment. She was awakened to the morning prayers and then taken to have breakfast with the other women living there. When she returned to her room, she saw how Shterna took a chair next to her door and sat there.

"Anything you need, you can ask me," said Shterna when she noticed Shayna staring at her.

What Shayna needed was to get out of there.

CHAPTER 19

ORTEGA

He reviewed a list of the certified kosher slaughterhouses that served most of the area. The knife found at the last crime scene had come from one of them. He was sure about it, but which?

Even though he had a hunch he would find some answers there, it was still a long shot. For now, however, he was eager to contact Rabbi Isaac Setzer, who had been so close with Abraham Lehrer the days before the crime. The police had already interrogated him but hadn't come up with anything. But, of course, they didn't. Finally, after a few phone calls, Ortega had managed to find his location: he was staying at a two-star hotel downtown. Wasting no time, he checked the place immediately. After asking for Setzer at reception and casually sliding a Benjamin Franklin over the desk, he was told: "Room 613. He specifically requested that room." Ortega thanked the concierge and went straight to the elevator when a tall man, completely dressed in black from toe to hat, appeared by him.

"Are you Isaac Setzer by chance?"

The man smiled back.

"I think my cover is blown."

"It has been for a while. I suggest you choose a better place for accommodation the next time you visit the town."

"I hope it is not anytime soon. I am still here because the police have asked me to stay. They are paying for these days I wasn't planning. As soon as they clear me, I'm heading back south."

The elevator arrived.

"Would you care to join me for a drink?" asked Ortega.

The rabbi smiled again.

"I should tell you, my friend, that I am straight."

"It is not about that."

"And what is it, then? I assume you aren't here to talk conversion either."

"No. I want to ask you some questions regarding the crime at Tikvah's youth center."

"And you are?"

Ortega gave him a personal card.

"Private Investigator. I am working for Margaret Wainstein. She was the mother of...."

"I know who Margaret Wainstein is," interrupted him Setzer.

"So?"

"I am a little tired of all these interrogations and shenanigans since the crimes, but I could also have a drink. And this hotel has a pretty decent bar."

They went to the hotel's bar, which was nothing fancy but seemed decent to Ortega's eyes.

They sat down. Ortega ordered a lemon tea while the rabbi asked for a glass of vodka.

"I always thought that religious people didn't drink," said Ortega, trying to ease things up.

"And I always thought Mexicans only drank tequila," said Rabbi Setzer.

"Well, you never stop learning."

"That is the beauty of life."

Ortega sipped his tea.

"Now, seriously, what do you want to ask me that the police haven't asked me yet?"

"Well, rabbi, I don't know what the police have asked you, but it seems that it has been of little help for them to solve this crime."

"So it seems," agreed Setzer as he poured the whole glass of vodka through his throat.

"Let's cut to the chase. What is your relationship with Rabbi Abraham Lehrer?"

"He is my friend. Well, he was my friend, I suppose, as now he is accused of these horrendous crimes. But, anyway, that is if he ever turns up again."

"What do you mean?"

Setzer looked confused.

"Would you befriend a killer?"

"No, I wasn't asking about that. I asked about the part where you suggested he might never turn up again."

"I don't know about his current whereabouts, but I think it is pretty clear he doesn't want to be found right now."

"So it seems."

"Then there is your answer. I don't think he will voluntarily appear in the district attorney's office."

"Did he ever say something that could point toward the crime he is now accused of?"

"What? Of course not. Everyone now thinks that all of us, Hasidim in Tikvah, are involved in crimes and other horrible things because of him. It is disgusting."

"You have to admit that in the last months, there have been two high-profile cases related to your people."

"And so many crimes have been committed by Mexicans and Chicanos like you. So are you going places accusing all of your people of being criminals?"

"Of course not."

"That is what I thought."

"Where were you the night of the crime?"

"At the crime scene, but I returned to my room before the — what would you call it... gruesome discovery?"

"Why did you get back earlier, if I may ask?"

"Sure, I had a serious need to go to the washroom."

"And you couldn't just use one at the Tikvah center?"

"I preferred to come back here. I wasn't feeling well at all."

"Are there any witnesses of you returning before the crimes were discovered?"

"I assume you could ask the concierge. I was back here around nine or a quarter past nine."

"I see."

Ortega knew that the fact that Setzer hadn't been at the crime scene at the moment of the revelation didn't mean he couldn't have helped Abraham Lehrer commit the crimes. The coroner's office had reported that the women had been killed at least six hours before their corpses were theatrically displayed to the crowd.

"Do you recall what you did during that day?"

"You mean before the party?"

"Exactly,"

"Well, of course, I put on my tefillin and said my prayers first thing in the morning. I spent the rest of the morning studying the Torah, had a light lunch, and then spent the rest of the afternoon studying until it was time to go to the party. You know, all those things you goyim consider boring."

"Where did you do all those things?"

Setzer looked perplexed.

"Here, in my hotel room, I had lunch in this same restaurant."

"I didn't know they serve kosher food."

"Of course, they serve kasher. If they didn't, I wouldn't stay here whenever I visit the city."

It had become clear to Ortega that there wasn't much he could take out from that man. He would check with the corrupt concierge if he effectively had been in his room all the day of the crime, but there wasn't much more he could do besides that.

"Now that we are on the topic, could you explain something about all this kosher thing?"

"Do you want me to explain why Coca-Cola is kasher?"

"I was thinking more about what makes a piece of meat kosher."

"For meat to be kasher, the cow must have been ritually killed by a shochet. First, he will cut the animal's throat with a single cut. This must be performed with a knife of around sixteen inches. The blade must have no marks when the animal's throat is cut with this knife. Then the shochet will verify that the animal does not show holes in its lungs or stomach; if it is fine, it is left to bleed."

Ortega was taking note of everything he was being told.

"Let me guess your next question: yes, Rabbi Abraham Lehrer is, in fact, a qualified shochet. He used to conduct ritual killings. Of animals, of course."

"Why are you telling me this?"

"Because I want you to find him. Everybody in Tikvah is eager for him to be finally caught so all this can end."

Ortega took out the list of the kosher slaughterhouses around the city he had.

"Could you tell me if Abraham Lehrer used to work in one of these?"

"Well, I am not entirely sure about this, but I can tell you that the only one that provides Tikvah is this one," he pointed to one name on the sheet of paper. "However, it has been out of business for over a month now."

"Why?"

"After the Wainstein tragedy, many businesses in our community became... not profitable. And if not, they have been quietly shut down by our leaders until all this passes away. That is also why we are eager to find the truth about these crimes."

"I see."

"You see now why we are so anxious that this horrible thing becomes clear?"

"One last question, if you don't mind, rabbi?"

"Sure. What is it?"

"Why do you keep saying 'kasher' when I say 'kosher'?"

The rabbi smiled again:

"It is the same word. We, Ashkenazi Jews, say kasher. It is in the Yiddish form. But they mean the same thing."

"Thank you for your time, Rabbi Setzer."

"My pleasure," said the man.

Ortega took off while the rabbi stayed at the table, ordering another glass of vodka for himself. He knew Setzer was lying or, at the bare minimum, holding information. But there was nothing else he could do at the moment.

Chapter 20

Shayna

Her days at the boarding school for Jewish girls were all similarly dull. Shayna had started to think that maybe, just maybe, her father was right, and this would be in her best interests. She knew it wouldn't take long to get used to that kind of life again. Religion still didn't mean the same as it had meant before. Inside that kasher bubble, she didn't need to worry about the killings and her dead sister. She didn't have to think of anything at all. She was about to resign herself to the happy monotony of every day being the same as the day before when something disturbing happened on the first Wednesday after she had arrived. She was resting in her bed, enclosed in her own private "jail cell," as she thought about the hotel-like bedroom she had been assigned when someone knocked on her door.

"This must be one of Rachel Buman's zealots here to take me to Rabbi Goldfarb's class," Shayna thought, surprised because, according to her calculations, the class wouldn't start until a few hours later. She walked to the door and opened it, expecting to see Shterna Daye or even Rachel Buman. Instead, she found a cardboard box with a simple card on top that read "Shayna." She looked at both sides of the hallway, trying to figure out if the person who had left the box would still be around, but nobody was there. She could quickly try to walk out of her room, through the hallway, to the staircases, and then to the boarding school's front door and try to catch the person who had left it there, but instead, she opted to stay. Shayna took the cardboard box at her feet and returned to her room, ensuring nobody had seen her. It was a small, rectangular, and slim box. She looked again at the card with her name and opened the box. Inside was a cell phone wrapped in a piece of folded paper. When she opened the paper, there was a letter for her. Shayna read,

B"H
Give it good use.

Signed: Someone who wants to help you.

That was it. Nothing else was there. She was perplexed. Who would have sent her a phone? And how could it help her? She took it in her hands and inspected it in all its parts. It was an expensive model, one that she had never touched before. She also could tell it looked exactly like a young Tikvah rabbi would use. She held it in her hands for a few seconds. Who should she call? Shayna would not call her dad or anyone in her family; apart from them, she didn't have many friends. Well, of course, there was Matt. He was the only person she had been in touch with recently outside Tikvah. And then she suddenly experienced a bad feeling. What if all this was just another test his father had arranged for her? What if she was being teased to call the *frei* just to mount the evidence that she was irredeemable? "Look, she is beyond anything we can do. We put her in the boarding school, filled her days with Torah studies, and ensured she followed Tikvah Zhytomyr's precepts. Despite that, she cannot be trusted!" she could imagine his father telling the community. She put the phone back into the box where it had come and hid it under her bed.

The rest of the day passed in the bucolic and monotonous calm of boarding school days. Then, on Thursday, she woke up feeling uneasy and decided to change her situation. She decided to take a chance with the phone again; she took it from the box and turned it on. It took little for her to learn to use it. It was pretty basic and designed so a child could learn in minutes. She passed through all the shining apps the phone had pre-installed until reaching the phone directory app. There it was: "Matthew." It was his number. How could he know she was in the boarding school? How could he have arranged for the phone to reach the door of her room? She would have to ask him. Shayna touched the name on the screen, and the phone started dialing. Outside the room, she heard one of her gatekeepers guarding the door. She would have to be very quiet to avoid being heard speaking with him. The phone rang three times before someone on the other end answered. It was a woman. She hung up the phone nervously. After a few seconds, she gave it another try. She was prepared this time, so when the same woman picked up the phone, she asked for Matt.

"Just a second, please," said the woman, and Shayna waited anxiously until she heard Matt's voice.

"Who is this?"

"Shayna,"

A short time passed in silence as if Matt was trying to remember who she was.

"Shayna!" he finally exclaimed. "Finally! I was worried about you. Haven't heard from you in a while."

"I just wanted to thank you for the gift," she said.

Another awkward, brief silence endured.

"What gift?"

"The cell phone," she said. "I am speaking to you from it right now. May I ask you how you got it to me?"

"Shayna, I do not know what you are talking about," he answered.

She had been right. It was all a trap from her father. She had been baited, and she had fallen for the bait.

"Can you give me a second, please? Don't hang up," he said. Shayna was about to do just that, to hang up, but then he talked again. "I am sorry for that. I just went out to the balcony to talk more easily. Could you explain to me what is going on? I have been trying to reach you for days, but I haven't been able to so far, and now you suddenly call me and thank me for a gift I could not possibly have given you. I am a little confused, you see. Anyway, it is good to hear from you. I have made some advances in the case I wanted to share with you."

"I am sorry, Matt, it will have to be at another time," said Shayna, sure that her father or one of his zealots had staged the whole situation to entrap her. "Please, wait for my call. Do not, by any means, try to reach me at this phone number."

"But..." he mumbled just before Shayna ended the communication.

She was now convinced she had to leave the boarding school.

CHAPTER 21

ORTEGA

Carlos Ortega had been sitting in his car outside the slaughterhouse for over three hours. He had not yet seen anything out of the ordinary. It was around noon, and it was an unusually sweltering day out there. He'd never seen a slaughterhouse before. Nonetheless, he assumed that, aside from the Hebrew letters on the front, this one looked like any other. It had been over three hours of him sitting there, waiting for something to happen or someone to enter the place, and yet, nothing. The quiet street was empty, and the sky was clear. He took a large breath and thought about some of his previous adventures. He hated to admit it, but the years had taken a toll on him. He wasn't the same as he had been. And yet, he was there, and he was ready to get back into action. He exited the car, crossed the street to the slaughterhouse's front door, and rang the bell several times. No one came to the door. He started walking around the outside of the building and found nothing unusual. The structure comprised four big white and grey walls enclosing a courtyard. He then returned to the front door and started ringing the bell again.

Once again, nobody responded. The place seemed abandoned. He walked a few steps back and looked back at the entire building. It was quite impressive. A concrete brutalist monster that stood among a set of crumbling, rusty, and abandoned factories. Gentrification hadn't reached that part of the city's outskirts yet. But Ortega knew it was just a matter of time before the entire neighborhood started changing into overpriced recycled housing and cafes for legions of hungry avocado toast eaters. He took another look at the building. Besides the entrance, there was a medium wall he knew he could climb and maybe inspect the place. And why not?

The place seemed as if it had been abandoned for quite some time so that it wouldn't hurt anyone. He made sure the street was empty and then started climbing the wall. It was not a simple task. He would have come better equipped if he had known that he would end up doing something like that. The plain soles from his shoes didn't help him get to the top of the wall, but in the end, he got there. He avoided the barbed wire and jumped into a courtyard full of rusty equipment and tools. In a corner, an open door led him to the interior. A stench of blood and death, the thick smell of cooling animal fat, and the scent of fresh meat and guts stung him immediately upon entering the building. He was now in a large room with four large cattle barrels muddied and slick with blood, bits of animal skin, and hair matted in the mud. They smelled of rust and oil. He had done some light research before venturing to the place. He knew those barrels were used in kosher ritual slaughtering. The cattle would be entered into one of those kinds of barrels, which then would make a 180-degree turn so that the animal's throat would end up facing the ceiling. The slaughter would then slit the throat. It was a nasty business. Surrounding the machines there slaughtering were small puddles of mud and rotten blood infested by flies. Nobody had taken the time to clean up the mess, and it all looked like it had been abandoned in a hurry. It was annoyingly disgusting. Ortega washed the sweat from his forehead with his hands. The combination of the heat inside the building and the rotten smell made his stomach ache. His heart was racing uncontrollably. He closed his eyes and counted to ten. When he opened them again, he felt a little better. Ortega walked down the hallway between the rows of slaughtering machines. A silver reflection caught his eye. Resting on the border of an enormous pool filled with more rotten blood and viscera, there was a ritual butcher knife like the one found at the crime scene. He took a few steps toward the ritual knife when he saw a flash of light reflected in his eye for less than a second. He immediately knew what was about to happen as a blade behind him went looking for his throat. Instinctively, he shrunk down, and the blade cut the air above where his throat had been. On his knees, Ortega reached for the ritual knife around two feet from him. But he was wrong and hadn't accounted for the agility of his attacker. An unexpected kick to his head knocked him onto the stone floor. He rolled to avoid another kick and ended up looking at the ceiling. A timid ray of sun coming in from one window was falling obliquely on the back of his attacker, covering in shadows his face and the rest of his body dressed in black. Apart from the long, curly lock of hair coming from the sides of his face, a pointy beard, and a black hat, Ortega couldn't make out any other details. Another kick reached Ortega's chest. It pushed all the air out of him and covered him with dust. His attacker was wearing fancy, well-polished black leather shoes. Another kick came Ortega's way, but he was able to stop it, grabbing the foot. He tried to bend it, and his attacker fell to the ground. Ortega got up, but the other probed to be more agile and had already recovered. He received Ortega with a direct cross to his jaw, sending the Mexican again to kiss the ground. He landed on his butt and took a hand to his lips, which were now bleeding. Ortega considered that the guy might have broken some fingers, judging by the force of the impact on his jaw. "Enough playing," he thought as he reached for his Browning. The shadowy figure realized it and ran away. Ortega's hand was a trembling mess, and he missed three shots. His attacker was now getting away. He stood up and started chasing him through the building. The man had a considerable advantage in his favor, and Ortega was still grasping for air. He saw the attacker passing a door with an "Exit" sign. He followed him and arrived at an office space. At least there, the air was easier to breathe, as there wasn't the awful stink of rotten viscera. His attacker was nowhere to be found. Ortega walked through the hallways. There was paperwork, boxes, and computers still running in the office. It was then obvious that the building had been suddenly abandoned. But why? He would have to think about that later. Meanwhile, he had lost his attacker's track. Ortega saw a door near a corner. He approached with caution, and the gun pointed. He opened the door with a sudden move. It was a small bathroom. A drop of sweat fell from the tip of his nose as if it were jumping off a trampoline. He saw another door at the other end of the room. He walked through piles of abandoned papers that lay on the ground. He opened the door and passed the gun to the other side first, followed by the rest of his body. It was another office, which looked more depressing and dark, with the only window covered in a blackout. A single metal file cabinet stood on a faded grey carpet in the middle of the room. There was no signal from the attacker.

"Come outside so we can talk," he said out loud. "I won't hurt you. You have my word."

Nobody answered. He was feeling ill, confused, and, frankly, uncomfortable. He had been in worse places, but there was something different about this one. Maybe it was the heat, or maybe it had been the smell of rotten blood and cow viscera splattered all around the slaughter yard, or maybe it was all those things combined. He inspected the room and went around the file cabinet. Ortega could not see any fresh blood trail or stain anywhere in the room, but it was hard to spot anything on the dirty grey carpets. He went back to the office space and walked in between the desks. Nothing. No traces of his attacker.

He then heard a door suddenly opening and closing. The sound came from the slaughter yard. He ran to the door, opened it, and went straight into the sight of that infernal butchering machinery. He went all the way to the end of the room. And then he noticed it. He hadn't seen it before because he had been attacked just when getting to that part of the slaughter yard. Now that the attacker had gotten away, Ortega could finally see it. See what the attacker might have tried to prevent him from seeing. He started to feel dizzy and tried to rest his body on the greasy walls. He slipped away and ended up on the floor. That same floor had been blackened by urine, shit, and blood. Yet, he couldn't look away from that butchering barrel. The naked body of a man inside the barrel was facing the ceiling, strapped as if it were a cow. His throat had been sliced, and blood poured slowly to the floor through his thick, long beard. A black Hasidic hat was the only thing he was wearing. Ortega took a big breath and got back to his feet. He inspected the corpse and looked at it with fascination and terror. If he was correct, and he had rarely been wrong in his life, it belonged to Rabbi Abraham Lehrer, the primary suspect in the Purim Massacre case.

CHAPTER 22

MATT

A news anchor and a pundit were discussing the recent crime at the slaughterhouse on his TV screen. His phone rang.

"Have you heard?" Margaret Wainstein's voice inquired.

"Yes, I was just watching it on the TV."

"Ortega is on it."

"I am aware."

"No, I mean, he discovered the body."

"I didn't know."

"Exactly. They are keeping it under the radar. That is why I am telling you."

"Umm, fine. Thank you."

"Just forget about this whole thing. It is way more dangerous than I thought when I first contacted you."

"It is fine. I have been researching myself just because I felt like it."

"That is why I insist you let this pass."

"That is all?"

"Yes."

"Then thank you for your call," he said, hanging up.

She was right that the situation had turned out to be far bloodier than he had expected, but it was too late for him to back down. He unmuted the TV. The news anchor was speaking on the phone with Rabbi Moshe Lehrer, Tikvah's leader and, if he recalled correctly, also Shayna's father. It was a rare sight, as he had refused, to this day, to give interviews. It was not very interesting either. The news anchor was trying to make him speak about the murders, his slain daughter, and his brother. Instead, he was dwelling on his life story, recalling how he had been a Zohar study prodigy as a young man and how he had rebuilt Tikvah after the death of their Rebbe. It was almost as if he was expecting something terrible to happen to him and trying to make a good name for himself before it did.

Matt thought that, even though he had the same long, thick beard and blue eyes as his recently deceased brother, this man looked much more serious and pious than Rabbi Abraham. Matt couldn't stop remembering his first encounter with Abraham Lehrer, how he had seemed like a goofy, chill, and joyous guy. He couldn't believe he'd committed the Purim murders, and now he couldn't believe he'd been murdered.

After Rabbi Moshe Lehrer was done bragging about himself, the news anchor said that another rabbi from a different Jewish congregation, Raoul Goldman, would call in. His voice seemed clear and soft, and it took him just a few minutes to disparage Tikvah and the Hasidic movement. First, he explained that the Hasidic approach to Judaism was sectarian. Then, the rabbi noted that the Vilna Gaon, a highly esteemed Talmudic sage from the eighteenth century, had twice previously excommunicated the Hasidim and all of their sects, once in 1771 and then again in 1778.

"Maybe it is time for a new ex-communication," said Goldman joyfully. He then talked about other global scandals involving Hasidim and Tikvah. Matt knew there had been serious theological arguments between Hasidic Jews and other, more mainstream forms of Judaism in the past. Still, all of those arguments had happened hundreds of years ago. Now, it seemed like Goldman was taking advantage of the situation to further push these long-forgotten theological discussions into the eyes of an unaware audience. Goldman was talking about how some Tikvah donors in Kenya had been involved in trafficking blood diamonds and how people got sick after being served spoiled kosher food at a Tikvah center in Madrid, Spain. Matt didn't hold Tikvah in a good light, but this was ridiculous. He googled the rabbi's name and was not surprised to find that he had transformed the webpage from his community into a full-scale propaganda machine against Tikvah. Apart from that, nothing else could interest Matt on the webpage, but he filled out a contact form anyway. He received a follow-up e-mail a few hours later. It stated that Rabbi Goldman was very busy and, unfortunately, could not meet him in the near future. Still, instead, it offered him to meet one of his students. "It seems like Rabbi Goldman is too busy grifting with the whole Tikvah debacle," he thought. Matt answered the e-mail saying he would be pleased to meet this so-called student. They set up a meeting for the following day at lunch.

When Matt arrived at the restaurant they had set, he was surprised to be met by a man in his mid-forties carrying a discrete yarmulke and dressed informally.

"I suppose you are Matt," the man greeted him.

"I am, and you are then...."

"Elijah Frenkel," said the other man, "I am one of Rabbi's Goldman students."

The man seemed nervous and sleazy.

"Please, join me," said Frenkel, pointing to the table where he had been waiting for Matt to arrive. "So, I recall you are interested in the work of Rabbi Goldman."

"I am curious, yes." He couldn't end his phrase when Frenkel interrupted him to ask what he was having for lunch.

"A green salad will be fine," said Matt, taking out a notepad. "Is it okay if I take notes?"

"Sure," said the other, calling the waitress to order their meals.

"So, what can I tell you about Rabbi Goldman's work?"

"Well, first, I would like to know how long you have been studying with him."

"You ask because you think I am a grown-up man, old enough to be a rabbi?"

"That would be an interesting starting point," remarked Matt.

"I know. I know. Well, I have just recently joined Rabbi Goldman's community. I have been a Jew all my life, but never cared a lot about it. And then, some things didn't go as I expected. In my life, you know? Women are the worst. And my ex is the worst of the worst. I don't want to bore you with stories about that bitch, but let's say she dumped me. So I was left on the street without access to our children or money. Rabbi Goldman was the only person who cared for me and helped me get back on my feet."

"It almost seems as if Rabbi Goldman was for you what Tikvah Zhytomyr has been for many others."

The man went pale.

"What are you suggesting?"

"Oh, nothing, really. Just as you found spiritual and material help from Rabbi Goldman and his community, many other Jews, even secular Jews like myself, have found the same with Tikvah."

"Well, you are wrong, young man. You're completely wrong. Rabbi Goldman's community has nothing to do with Tikvah or its teachings. We are a happy community. They are a sect, a twisted sect of lunatics. And I am telling you firsthand as I met them before being rescued by Rabbi Goldman."

"I see. Could you tell me more about your experience?"

"Well, yes, I could. But to what end? As I said, I began transiting a dark path once my wife dumped me. That was when these people approached me. They have like a radar for Jews in despair. They don't do it because they care but because they want to recruit cannon fodder to help them commit crimes!"

"I see."

"Yes, I can tell you that. I even got to know the guy."

"Which guy?"

"The guy. The man that killed his wife and his children!"

"You mean David Wainstein?"

"He went by the name Nathan Wainstein when I met him."

"Fine, and how did you get involved with him and Tikvah in the first place?"

"As I was saying, I was in despair once the bitch I married left me around seven years ago. Then, one Friday afternoon, I was walking on the street downtown when a teenager approached me. Yes, a teenager. Can you believe it? They exploit their children to lure innocent people into their horrible, twisted sect."

"And what did this teenager say to you?"

"He asked me if I had put the tefillin that day. Of course, I hadn't. I was far from a religious person then. But the kid knew I was a Jew just by my looks. I will give that to them. They are incredible at detecting Jews in the street. So I told him that I had never put on the tefillin. At first, the child seemed shocked, but he rapidly helped me put them on and told me I had officially concluded my Bar Mitzvah. I was a little confused, but he told me that effectively, the first time you put the tefillin, it is considered your Bar Mitzvah. So, I was intrigued. He then asked me if I had plans for that Shabbos night. I had not. I was probably going to get back home and watch some TV before going to bed. But, even though I didn't know these people, the idea of spending the night with them was appealing. So I accepted. If I remember well, he took me to the house of a rabbi named Gorowitz. That night seemed nice, and so I started attending their events. That is how I got to know Nathan or David Wainstein, as you wish to call him."

"But there was something that took you away from Tikvah."

"Yes, well, of course! In the beginning, it all seemed pretty mild. I went to the meeting but didn't wear my black coat and hat. They didn't expect me to start eating kosher in my private life yet. Their only requirement was that I wore a yarmulke when with them. It seemed easy, and honestly, it didn't bother me."

"It still seems pretty normal."

"Well, yes. That will always be their public face. But behind curtains, there was a lot of nasty in-fighting. I only got to see a glimpse of that. However, what turned me off was their obsession with the coming of the Messiah turned me off. These people were obsessed with that! And, while they would not admit it to strangers, they were convinced that their late Rebbe was the Messiah, that he would rise from the dead and reveal to the world that he was the Jewish Messiah. And, my friend, what else would you call a religion that holds that a dead Jew will rise from the dead and show the world that he is the Messiah but Christianity?"

"I see."

"That is when I started to question their teachings. I looked for different answers, and I was lucky to find Rabbi Goldman, who understood what I had been through and lent me a hand. He was different. He cared for me and my problems. My experience with Tikvah was that they were more interested in me as a number, a performer of mitzvot instead of a human being. Tikvah believes every Jew has the mission to perform mitzvot to make the world more sacred. Once the world is sacred enough, the Messiah will show himself or resurrect from his tomb. They won't explicitly admit they believe in that, but they do. I find it frankly sacrilegious to Judaism."

"So that is the reason you left Tikvah."

"Primarily, yes., but also because certain rumors were going around. Some nasty stuff I didn't like at all."

"Could you please be more explicit?"

The man seemed uncomfortable by Matt's question.

"You know," he said, "I feel you are more interested in me talking about Tikvah Zhytomyr than about the work of Rabbi Goldman."

"It is just only that I got to know Rabbi Goldman because of his opinions on Tikvah. And I am just curious as I decide which way to take my faith." He knew this phrasing would work as Tikvah and Goldman competed for the same Jews as him.

"Fine. I don't want to go much deeper, but there were rumors about a group inside Tikvah that had split from the main branch and gone rogue. And now we're witnessing all these crimes, so there was some truth to that."

"Do you know anything more about that?"

"To be frank, no. I only recall hearing something about 'The Bleeding Star.' I suppose that was the name the group had taken, but apart from that, I didn't get involved. I abandoned Tikvah shortly after."

Matt knew he couldn't get the man to tell him anything else worthwhile, so he asked some general questions about Goldman's mission and made a reason to leave. At least he had a name now, "The Bleeding Star," whatever the hell that was supposed to mean.

CHAPTER 23

ORTEGA

H e wiped the sweat from his forehead with the sleeve of his shirt. He confirmed his suspicion. The body over there was of Abraham Lehrer. He felt lucky that he had escaped the same fate, although barely. The stench of rotten blood and meat, the insane heat, and the massacred corpse made him feel like he was living in a *Texas Chainsaw Massacre* film. He looked back at the crime scene. A ray of sunlight reflected on a spot beside the corpse through one of the top windows. A continuous, thin line of blood dripped over a silver coin. He took it and examined it under the light of the sun. It was large and heavy, prompting a carved star of the Jews on both sides. He put it into his pocket. He went outside, took a deep breath, got into his car, and drove to a bar. He asked the bartender for a beer and a phone. The man pointed him to an old public booth that was still active, as if the last fifteen years had never happened. He called 911, told about the corpse in the slaughterhouse, and then hanged when the questions began. Ortega returned to the counter, took his ordered beer, and drank it in one large sip. He asked for another one and then another one. It was as if he was dehydrated. The barman looked at him suspiciously. It was not even four in the afternoon, and the bar was empty apart from him and a drunken man sleeping on the opposite end of the counter. Ortega paid for the beers, included a generous tip for the barman, and went out.

Back in the office, he called Margaret Wainstein and told her what he had seen. She listened silently and told him to keep her informed before hanging up on him. Ortega then lit a Cuban cigar, letting himself loose on the dusty, green sofa he occasionally used as a bed. The barking of a dog woke him up the next day. His head felt like it would explode, and his whole body was aching. He went straight to the small bathroom, evacuated, shaved, and brushed his teeth. It was a new day, and he had a lot of things to do. Once in the street, he bought a copy of each newspaper, returned to the car, and drove to a nearby cafe. He had a San Pellegrino and a sandwich while going through the newspapers. Except for one tabloid, the news of the crime had not made it to the front page but had been relegated to the crime section. All of them said more or less the same. The police seemed to know nothing about what had happened. There was no mention of his name. He now had to visit Rabbi Isaac Setzer once again.

CHAPTER 24

MATT

The Marshall Blum Center's librarian had left a message on his cell phone asking him to come by.

It was five in the afternoon, just minutes from the library closing its doors to the public. Matt entered the center and walked through the large hallway that ended at the library's glass door. Debra was sitting, as always, behind her desk, going through the books that had been returned that day. She barely moved her eyes from the PC screen while Matt walked to the desk.

"I have something that might interest you," she said directly.

"That is what you told me on the phone."

"Give me a second while I finish the paperwork. Take a seat."

He went through the shelves filled with books and felt that time had stopped. He often experienced that feeling while there. The place was warm and intimidating, filled with the smell of thousands of dusty books and the buzzing of a hundred old lamps. He sat down at a table close to Debra's desk, waited for her to finish her work, and then she came over to sit in front of him with a notepad.

"I have been researching your thing, the blood libels, and all that."

"My thing, you call it?"

"I think this will interest you," she replied, ignoring his comment and pointing to his annotations with the tip of a pen. "Place yourself in the north of France. It is the year 1191 in a tiny community called Bray. A nobleman murders a Jew. Why, you may ask? The answer is simple: 'Why not?' These kinds of things were common during medieval times. Well, maybe not only in medieval times. The thing is that the Jewish community in Bray asks the Countess that she allows them to take vengeance upon the aristocrat. For unknown reasons, she accedes. Do you follow?"

Matt nodded. Debra pointed with the tip of her pen to another line in his annotations.

"Great," she said, "the thing then is that the Jewish community of Bray, with the explicit permission of the Countess, grabbed this aristocrat and started dragging him through the streets. They may have been a little too festive or too immersed in the carnival spirit, given that it was Purim, and they punished this man by putting a crown of thorns on his head. You have seen how Purim goes. People get drunk, and people usually go over the top occasionally. But you also have to consider that Purim is a festivity when we Jews celebrate the triumph over Haman. This ancient king almost got all of our ancestors killed. An old Purim tradition, one that has thankfully been ditched, was to make effigies of Haman that then they would crucify and burn."

"Like the burning man of medieval times?" asked Matt.

"Something like that, but with fewer hipsters and more peasants. What do you think would be the issue with this custom?"

"I don't know. Maybe people would think those effigies represented Jesus instead of Haman?"

"Bingo. This tradition did not amuse Gentiles. They considered it blasphemous, offensive, and, frankly, another proof that Jews were evil. So, returning to this fool aristocrat who was chased and killed by a group of Jews, when the King of France heard about it, he found a great reason to kill all of Bray's Jews and take their land. He followed through, and on March 18, 1191, eighty Jews were burnt at the stake by his order."

"That is a horrifying story."

"At least the king spared the lives of every male Jew of less than thirteen years that had yet to have their Bar Mitzvah. Although, the condition was that they converted to the Christian faith."

"So, for now, we have the fake crucifixion and a crown of thorns. What else do you have for me?"

Debra smiled.

"I knew you would expect more than this. Let's get back in time a little further now. According to Roman historian Socrates of Constantinople, a Christian child was crucified by Jews in the year 415. It happened during Purim as well. But there is even more. During the 15th century, there was this idea that a blood transfusion from a healthy child could save the life of a sick person. In 1492, the blood of a young Jewish boy was used to try to save the life of Pope Innocent VIII, but it didn't work. The pontiff died as a result. You can imagine the rest."

"Well, that is an impressive account."

"Wait, there is more. One of the most infamous cases that involved blood libel happened in 1144 in Norwich, England. According to Thomas of Monmouth, a child, William of Norwich, was kidnapped, tortured, and crucified by a group of Jews. Monmouth's accusations ignited a series of antisemitic attacks, ending with the expulsion of all the Jews from England in 1290. It also helped ignite the whole blood libel thing. Two ideas conform to the basic blood libel. First, the idea of the blood. This means that Jews replaced Jesus Christ with Christian blood. In their twisted vision, Jews know Christians are right and use the blood of Christians to perform cabalistic rituals and things of the sort. Then, there is the idea of ritual killing. As I showed you, it was first associated with Purim's festivity. Still, with time, it would be associated with Pesach, which almost always falls around the same time as Easter. This is important because the blood libels make it look like the Jews mock the passion of Christ."

"Like kneading the matzah with blood?"

"Exactly. Like 'Pesach is coming, and we must start kneading the matzah.' Wasn't something like that the message found in the Purim crime scene? Only Christian blood is being discussed. Used for baking matzah and satanic rituals to consecrate communion wafers."

Matt felt shivers down his spine.

"Please, go on."

"I could go on, of course. Unfortunately, blood libels have been a constant during much of Jewish history. It is an extended tradition founded on vile lies that have always been about demonizing the Jewish people. For example, many people still believe that Jews get together yearly to sacrifice a Christian victim during Pesach and consecrate it to Satan or some shit like that."

"Almost like the annual sacrifice of a virgin to the Minotaur in Greek mythology."

"Yes, there is something on the order of the atavistic and death instinct. Another horrible case I wanted to tell you about is the one of Little Saint Hugh of Lincoln, also in England. I will spare you the details, as you can read them in *The Prisoner's Tale*, one of Chaucer's *Canterbury Tales*. In the story, he mentions the little Saint Hugh and goes on a long parade of nonsense about Jewish children's sacrifices."

She guessed Matt's following comment, and before he could say anything, she stated,

"Don't worry; I have put aside a copy of the book for you to take home. Keeping with the high literature, there is also a play, *The Innocent Child of La Guardia*, by one of Spain's Golden Age big names, Lope de Vega. Even though I am not an expert on Spanish theatre, I can tell you that this play is based on another false accusation of Jewish guilt. The poor accused confessed under torture by inquisitors, although the child's body was never found. Speaking of Spain, you can always count on noted anti-Semite Gustavo Adolfo Becquer for this kind of filth. He wrote about the case of the La Guardia child in one of his legends. I could go on for hours. I could tell you about other cases, all invented to generate hate against the Jews: Gabriel of Białystok, Simon of Trent, and the case of Menahem Mendel Beilis from Kyiv, a Jews unjustly accused of ritual murder of a Christian child in 1913. There is a harrowing novel by Bernard Malamud about the case, *The Fixer*."

"So, any of these cases were proved real?"

Debra's mouth curved into a sardonic grin.

"Of course not. This is all nonsense. All these were imaginative inventions put together to justify the persecution of Jews. No true Jew could ever get involved in such horrific acts. And there is a straightforward Talmudic reason: Jewish religion prohibits any form of ritual sacrifice. The Jewish sages forbade them after the destruction of the Second Temple."

"And couldn't it be the case that a Jewish sect would continue making sacrifices?"

"I have never come across something like that. So, all I can say is that if a Jew ever took part in a religious or ritual sacrifice, he would have been a bad Jew and a troubled person."

"So the question remains: why members of Tikvah are taking these fictional antisemitic myths into real human sacrifices?"

"That is up to you to discover. But wait for a second. I have one more small thing that could help. I saw something about it in a small pamphlet. It's not in any other book or encyclopedia that I've seen. It's about an accusation of blood in February 1753. You know where?"

"Let me guess, Zhytomyr?"

"You are dead right. Little Halina Brunnow. She disappeared from her home and was never found again. As I told you, little information is available on her case. According to the author of the pamphlet, Simon Plantick, the most probable explanation is that the girl's mother went out with her to the forest. They might have been looking for firewood since it was the middle of winter. The mother got distracted and left little Halina alone for a moment. Perhaps she was meeting someone and didn't want the girl to know. It's not clear. When she got back to her, she found the girl had been killed and eaten by wolves. In despair, the mother returned to town. She knew that if she told the truth about what had happened to her daughter, she would be held responsible and probably killed. So, what did she do? The easiest thing to do, she blamed the Jews in town."

Debra finished her explanation, and they went into a tense silence momentarily.

"Well, that is enough for one day. Don't you think?"

"Yes, it is more than enough," said Matt.

"Here, take the selection of works I told you about," said Debra, pointing to a pile of books by Chaucer, Malamud, Lope de Vega, and Becquer.

Matt thanked her for all she had done for him, took the books into his bag, and went out. But, before crossing the library's door, he remembered.

"Debra, one more thing. Have you ever heard something about a sect inside Tikvah called 'The Bleeding Star' or something like that?"

She gave it a quick thought and then answered that she had never heard about any sect named like that, nor inside Tikvah or any other Jewish congregation.

"Let me do some research on that."

"Are you sure?"

"Why not? That I haven't encountered this before is not proof that it doesn't exist."

He thanked her once again and went back home.

CHAPTER 25

ORTEGA

O rtega arrived at the hotel at noon, went directly to the reception, and asked for Setzer. The concierge, different from the one he had spoken to the last time, typed something on his computer and replied that the rabbi had already left two days ago. Ortega checked his notes and saw that Setzer had checked out the same day he had interviewed him.

"May I ask you at what time he checked out? I am an old friend of Rabbi Isaac and am worried about him. He has been experiencing some health issues lately. Early dementia, to be more specific. His doctor recommended that his closest friends look closely at his whereabouts. In case he ends in places where he shouldn't, you know."

The concierge didn't seem impressed initially, but he agreed anyway. After looking at the screen, he told Ortega that Setzer had done a "late check-out," leaving his room at four in the afternoon. That was just an hour after their meeting.

"Thank you for your cooperation. I know this might seem like an overreach, but is there any chance I could see the hotel's security tapes for the lobby and any other door to the exterior? His friends and I are apprehensive about his behavior on March 6. I don't know if you remember, but that day there was a horrific crime, and well, we are worried that he might have witnessed something, and now his life could be in danger. But, unfortunately, he wouldn't tell us."

"Well, this is highly irregular, and I may not grant you that kind of request," said the concierge.

"I know, I know, that is why I wanted to see if this could help," said Ortega, sliding a few Benjamins over the counter. The concierge took them so fast that it seemed like they had never been there.

"In that case, I am having lunch in fifteen minutes. Sometimes, I like to have it in the room beside me, where all the security recordings are stored. Greg, who works back there, appreciates it when I do that, as it allows him to take some minutes to smoke outside. So come back in fifteen minutes, and I will see what I can do," said the concierge.

Ortega took it to the bar, asked for a beer, and drank it in a few sips until fifteen minutes had passed. Then, he went back to the reception. "Come with me," told the concierge as he walked toward a small room behind.

"Lina will take my place in the reception," said the man, "but we have little time until Greg returns. So, you were looking for our tapes from March 6?"

"Front door and any other door where anyone inside the hotel could have reached the street," said Ortega.

"Let's see," said the concierge, sitting in front of a wall of monitoring screens. He put the date into a computer, and the recordings for that day came up on the screen in front of him. The screen started showing everyone entering and exiting the hotel through the front door and a lateral door for employees at fast-forward speed. Then, Ortega saw Rabbi Setzer exiting through the front door. It was impossible to miss him: a large, tall man dressed in black from head to toe. "Stop it there!" he asked the concierge. "What time was this?" The concierge checked the timestamp: "Fifteen past ten in the morning," he replied. Ortega checked his notes once again. "Ok, go on," he said. The rest of the tape was identically dull. Nothing was unusual until they saw the rabbi re-entering the hotel. This time, it had been at twenty to four in the afternoon. After checking his annotations once again, Setzer's alibi checked out. He thanked the concierge, left the hotel, and returned to his office. He sat down at the desk to think about his next step. By now, Setzer would probably be back at El Paso, and he couldn't do much about it. Ortega then remembered that he had taken a strange coin from the slaughterhouse. He reached into his pocket and retrieved the item, placing it on the desk. Nothing he had seen before. It had the portrait of the star of the Jews on both sides, but there was something more. A kind of tiny drop fell from each tip of the star. Could it be a forging mistake? After fiddling with the coin for a minute, he noticed a tiny drop of blood on one point of the star. And then he had a crazy idea. What if those drops in the metal were to represent, precisely, blood? Then, the coin would have a portrait of a bleeding star on each side.

CHAPTER 26

MATT

M att took a break from the PC screen. He had been reading Wikipedia for hours, going through the rabbit hole of Jewish orthodoxy and Hasidism. He was exhausted but at least had found some exciting information about a seventeen-century rabbi named Sabbatai Zevi, born in Izmir, in current-day Turkey. During his lifetime, this Zevi character claimed to be the Jewish Messiah. Many impoverished Jews believed him to the point of selling their few possessions to join him in his quest to overthrow the Sultan of Constantinople. Other sages from his time had also given him their blessings. One of such was Nathan of Gaza, who had predicted that Zevi would unify the ten lost tribes of Israel and topple the sultan.

The times of Zevi also coincided with pogroms around Europe and the rise of the Cossacks, who had been particularly sadistic against Jewish communities in Eastern Europe. These sufferings had brought many people to Zevi's herd under his promise of better times under his guidance. Matt had also read some people had been convinced that Zevi would bring them to Israel mounted in a cloud, and once there, he would rebuild the Temple of Jerusalem. It sounded like crazy talk, but at least the people who believed in this had lived during the 1666s. Now, he had met people in modern times who believed a dead man would resurrect and be crowned Messiah. In Matt's opinion, there wasn't a big difference between those beliefs. Unfortunately for the poor, gullible Jews that followed him, the grand revelation of Zevi had ended abruptly when, upon entering Constantinople to topple the sultan, he was detained for treason and given the option of the death penalty or conversion to the Muslim faith. After careful consideration, Zevi chose conversion for himself and his closest followers. It was a devastating blow to the impoverished Jews who fled their European homes to join him, dreaming of a future full of glory. However, some of Zevi's most devoted followers refused to accept that they had been conned and continued to believe he was the Jewish Messiah. To them, he was a master liar who had just fooled everyone, including the sultan, so that he could continue his holy mission. Matt was especially interested in the guy because some scholars thought that some sects that had split up because of all the trouble were still going strong today. Furthermore, some Hasidic groups were profoundly impacted and influenced by Zevi's interest in the Kabbalistic secret art and in performing miracles. Matt could certainly see similarities between the Sabbateist movement and Tikvah with their extreme faith in an imminent revelation of a Jewish Messiah and their unbounded proselytism.

He had a feeling that this could be a lead. But he also needed someone with a deeper understanding of the matter, so he e-mailed Debra, asking her for her opinion. Then he stood up and went to the balcony. It was already spring, but the weather was still cold and cloudy. He was feeling melancholic. What was all that about? What was he doing? Was he doing something that would help him figure out what happened to David? He stood on the balcony for an hour, looking at the people living their everyday lives, minding their business. Then, when the sun started falling, he felt the cold on his skin and decided to get inside. He was not hungry but prepared himself a sandwich anyway and filled the pot of Minerva with wet cat food. He went to bed and tried to read a mystery novel but quickly found that he was not in the mood, so he turned off the lights and fell asleep. The following day, around 9 a.m., an incoming e-mail woke him up. He sleepwalked to the PC and checked the screen. It was from Debra; in the subject field, he read: "Bingo."

Chapter 27

Ortega

He got into the subway and went all the way uptown. It was hot as hell down there as people filled every free spot during peak hour. When he finally reached his destination, only a black woman and her son were still riding the train. He waved his hand to the boy; the woman whispered something into his child's ear, and they took off, trying not to look at Ortega.

He exited the train at the next stop and returned to the surface. The sun hurt his eyes. He walked a few steps until he reached the Latin bar across the street. The outside was filled with kitsch colorful lettering. Still, inside, it was dark and depressing, almost as if it had never been changed in the forty years it stood in that corner. And that was probably the case. He went to the countertop. The bartender, a short and round brown guy with a mustache who appeared to have recently returned from serving in Pancho Villa's *Division del Norte* army, asked what he would have.

"Where can I find *Rubberface*?" said Ortega.

The bartender looked at him with curious eyes.

"Who is looking for him?"

"Name's Carlos Ortega. I am an old friend of his."

"Oh," said the bartender, "let me check." He rubbed his hands on his apron and disappeared through the back door.

Ortega waited a few minutes until the man returned and motioned for him to go that way. He walked through the back door, down a long hallway, and past a room where a numb young woman was watching a rickety television playing a *corrido*. He reached the end of the hallway and knocked on a wooden door before opening it.

"What's up, my *carnal*?" greeted him, a man with smallpox scars all over his face. They got into a hug.

"*Cara de goma*!" said Ortega, pulling the man apart. "It has been a long time."

"For sure! Come on in, come on in. Take a seat. Do you want something to drink? I have *Corona*. I know you like that shit!"

Ortega smiled.

"It is the *raza*, my friend. You know how it goes deep inside me."

"I am much more *raza* than you and wouldn't drink that cat's piss even if nothing else existed. Well, maybe only if that was the case."

Ortega sat on the chair in front of the man's desk.

"So, to what do I owe your visit, *mi amigo*?" said the other, sitting on a big chair with *faux leather* covering all cracked up.

"I want to go straight to the business if you don't mind."

"So, no *chela* for you?"

"No, thank you. I prefer not to drink when on duty."

Rubberface looked at him in all seriousness for a few seconds and then burst into laughter.

"Come on, *mi* friend. Don't talk shit to me. I have known you for twenty years. Your lies won't walk here."

"I have more pressing things in my mind right now," said Ortega. "I want to be sober as much as I can."

"Now, that is different. Do you see? No need to lie to your old friend, José."

Ortega took the silver coin he had found in the slaughterhouse out of his pocket and put it on the desk.

"Do you know something about this?"

Rubberface opened a drawer and frantically searched inside until he found a monocle. He put it on and looked at the coins.

"This is strange. Never seen something similar." He put the coin back on top of the desk.

"Could you keep it for a few days and see if something comes up?"

Rubberface took the coin and played with it between his fingers.

"Yeah, I suppose I could try to move it. Where did you get it?"

"Long story."

"Well, give me the short version."

"It was the Jews."

"Jews?"

"You know, the ones that have been on the news lately? Because of the killings?"

Rubberface went white.

"Oh, I want nothing to do with that *chingadera*. Take your shit coin and get out of here."

"Come on, José. You owe me."

"Yes, I owe you and can pay you in cash, but I don't want to get involved with that twisted shit."

"I am only asking you to see if you can find it a buyer. So you find me one, and I will handle the rest. And I will give you a five percent."

"Twenty," responded *Rubberface* rapidly.

"You see? *Hablando se entiende la gente*. I will give you seven."

"Fifteen is the minimum I will accept for putting myself in harm's way."

"What harm is in the way?"

"Maniacs! You know we are talking about Jewish maniacs!"

Ortega gave it a thought. He cared little about the money. He only wanted to get back into something he could use in the case, and this was his best shot.

"Fine, I will give you fifteen percent."

"That's it, *amigo*! It's always a pleasure doing business with you."

"Yeah, whatever you say." Ortega was ready to leave the room when *Rubberface* said to his back.

"By the way, you might want to visit these other guys. Some weird Christians have just arrived in the neighborhood and have already mounted one of those big, flashy churches."

"And why do you think I would be interested in some protestants? Not that I have suddenly gained an interest in the fate of my soul after my time on Earth."

"You are so funny. You know, that's your problem. You always let your desire to look smart get the best of you. You make it your whole life, so you don't notice the little things."

"Come on now, tell me why I would be interested in these other guys."

"Well," said *Rubberface,* savoring the moment, "they are not your usual protestants for once. Instead, they sell themselves as a mixture of Jewish and Christian values."

"I'm still not convinced why I should hang out with even more religious zealots."

"You see them for yourself. Have I ever told you something that was not worth at least checking?"

"I can think of a few things, certainly."

"They have their church a few miles from here." *Rubberface* searched the drawer in his desk again until he found an advertising flyer. "Here, take it."

Ortega took the paper and read: "Church of the Revived Messiah." It certainly was something he could tell by the sight of a David's Star superimposed on a Christian cross.

He reached the street and felt the sun again, aiming at his eyes. What now? He would have to wait at least a week to hear from *Rubberface,* and he hadn't thought of anything else. Maybe he could see what all that thing about the Revived Messiah was about. *Rubberface* had been correct that it was just a mile away. He could get back into the subway or walk. Living in a big city like that was full of opportunities to walk, something he found annoying and amazing at the same time. But he was getting old and knew he wasn't getting enough exercise to keep his body from falling apart. So he told himself, "What the hell, why not?" and walked through the barrio to the big church. Children ran yelling down the sidewalks, some without adult supervision, as their parents chatted with neighbors. The Latino markets had big signboards advertising all kinds of tamales, empanadas, and, more recently, arepas, which had come along with the last wave of Venezuelan immigrants. Ortega hadn't been there in a while, and he remembered that the chaos, noise, and bright colors were why he didn't want to go back.

He arrived at the mega-church. Although "mega" was an overstatement, it took up much less than a whole square, and its parking lot was small and almost empty. But still, it was a weekday, and it was around 4 p.m. He wondered how many people went to church on a typical Sunday. Few, judging by the number of parking spots.

He entered the building while a service was being held. It was just the pastor and a few faithful. Ortega sat at the back and patiently waited until the sermon was over. He looked at the place; the walls were covered with portraits of what he deemed sages. Or were they Saints? He knew little about Protestantism, being raised Catholic and not having attended mass or entered a Church for years. Still, he knew protestants don't worship saints, so it had to be some sage. "Well," he said to himself, "I might be dammed, but I am sure that the portrait of that guy over there belongs to Saint Augustine." And then he walked through the other portraits. They were all saints he recognized from his years of involvement in the Catholic church. He recognized Saint Expedite and Saint Anthony. There was, of course, a picture of the Virgen de Guadalupe, which was expected in that neighborhood.

He looked at the altar. The pastor was giving his sermon, and behind him, a giant human-sized cross. Around half the cross and just around a foot in front, there was a silver star of the Jews. That was odd but consonant with what he had seen on the flyer. One portrait, in particular, was hard for him to place. It showed a middle-aged man with neat facial hair and a tube-shaped turban. There was another portrait next to this one that Ortega did not know. It was a carbon portrait of a man with a scarf around his neck, wearing a fur hat and a tidy mustache just below his pointy nose. The man in the portrait was also dressed in what Ortega identified as an overcoat with printed feathers.

"You are not from around here," heard Ortega as he looked at the portraits. He had been so concentrated on coming up with the Saints in the paintings that he hadn't realized the sermon was over, and the pastor was now sitting beside him.

"I am sorry. Yes, this is my first time here, reverend."

"Pastor Salvador Hinojosa, at your service. It is always good to see new *hermanos* coming here."

"This is something completely new for me."

"Let me guess. You were raised a Catholic?"

"Yes, but apart from that, it is the Saints in the walls, and then the Jewish star you have on the altar... it all seems odd."

"We hear that a lot, but there is a good explanation for all. We are protestants, yes, but not traditional protestants. First, the Star of David. I assume this amazes you the most. Our Messianic Church respects and admires our bigger brothers, the Jews. We even count on a lot of Jews in our parish."

"Hard for me to believe."

"But it is true. Don't forget that Jesus Christ was himself Jewish! We follow the Torah and New Testament teachings at the Revived Messiah Church. We accept that the Jewish are God's chosen people and that his son, Yeshua or Jesus, is how God has extended his love to all other peoples who are not Jewish."

"I suppose traditional Jews don't look very kind to you and your Church."

"There will always be people who don't like us, but as I told you before, more and more *traditional Jews* who are unhappy with how things are going over there have recently joined us."

"You mean...?"

"No need for details, but I am sure you know things have been heating lately. There was a lot of hate and persecution against good people. Let's not talk about that. It is a horrible thing."

Ortega was almost equally fascinated and annoyed by the reverend.

"So, you believe in the teachings of the Jews, but also Jesus Christ, you are protestant but worship Catholic Saints? Is that correct?"

"That is an extremely simple way to see our theology, but overall... yes."

"I see. Well, I think I might better be going."

"You are welcome here anytime, *hermano*."

Ortega started walking toward the entrance. It had probably been a waste of time. He then realized he still knew nothing about those other two portraits hanging on the walls that had caught his attention. He turned around and said,

"One last thing, reverend Hinojosa, could you please explain to me whose Saints are those in these two effigies?" he said, pointing to the portraits.

"These?" said Hinojosa. "Oh, they are two Jewish sages. The first one was a mystic and a great man. His name was Sabbatai Zevi. The other corresponds to one of his disciples, Jakob Frank."

Ortega thanked the reverend and got out of there.

CHAPTER 28

MATT

M att opened Debra's email with a sense of excitement.

Hello Matt, I hope this e-mail finds you well. If not, I am sure it will prompt you to feel better. At least, that's what I think. So, let me get straight to the point. In your last e-mail, you mentioned Sabbatai Zevi. And when I read that, something clicked inside my head. Since Hasidism came to be, they have been "accused" of having ties to Sabbatai Zevi and the Sabbateist movement. So I looked at the Tikvah entry in the Encyclopedia Judaica, the 2007 edition, which is the latest. I just wanted to make sure you missed nothing.

I found no new leads there. Then I read the entry on Sabbatai Zevi, and again, nothing helpful there as well. Still, I felt that there was something I was missing in the greater scheme of things. I was sure I had seen a bleeding Maguen David or a "Bleeding Star," as you said, somewhere before. I spent the rest of the day thinking about that and trying to remember where I had seen something that could resemble a star with blood or something similar. Finally, at six, when I was closing the library's doors for the day, I took another look at the Encyclopedia Judaica. This time I took the 1972 edition for no reason other than having it closer to me at that moment. I checked once again the entries for Tikvah and Sabbatai Zevi. They said more or less the same, with some different wording, but nothing new. The only exception was that Zevi's entry mentioned one of his followers, Jakob Frank. I read it, and it was interesting and all, but what caught my attention was a portrait of the guy. I scanned it for you so that you can look.

Notice something out of the ordinary? Because I did. Look at the upper left side. It seems like something is off. I cannot tell how I noticed it, but it was there. So I zoomed in and found something rather curious. It is half of a bleeding Maguen David. I then went back to the Tikvah entry in the Encyclopedia. Still a dead end. I then tried one last thing, the entry for Joseph of Lemberg, Tikvah's first "Rebbe." There was a painting of him as well. Here, look at the good old man.

So, once again, I got the feeling that something was off in the picture. So I magnified it and went through it pixel by pixel until I found what I sought. Look at his tallit, and you will find it. It is the other half of a bleeding Maguen David. I assembled it for you. Look:

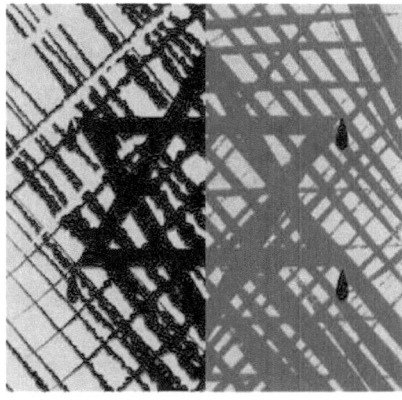

Mind-blowing, don't you think? So now we have further proof that there seems to be some kind of bond between Sabbatai Zevi's disciple, Jakob Frank, and Tikvah. I tried looking for the artist that did the paintings but couldn't find a name in the Encyclopedia, nor its webpage. I even tried phoning the publishing house in England. After a long time, I could speak with one editor. He had no idea what I was talking about and told me that the 1972 editors would have probably just used random paintings they dug up. He didn't think the publishers would have commissioned those portraits to an artist. So that is that. But there is more. I was surprised to learn that in 1759, Frank, his followers, and a group of the best Talmudic sages of the time held a theological debate in Lemberg. The debate took place in the city's cathedral. Frank may have been trying to get the head of the Catholic Church to protect him and his followers. You need to know that Jakob Frank was a con man and a charlatan. He tricked his people into thinking he was the real Messiah, leading them to commit sin actively. Yes, you read that right. His theology was a mixture of Catholicism and Jewish traditions with an emphasis on leading a sinful life to prompt the end of times. Crazy, right? Finally, he and his followers embraced the Catholic faith. They got baptized when they realized they would probably end dead if they continued with their shenanigans. Pretty similar to how Sabbatai Zevi also renounced his Jewish faith and converted to Islam when confronted by the Sultan. Getting back to that theological discussion in which Frank took part in 1759 at Lemberg, one of the key aspects of the debate that day was whether the blood libels were real. Jakob Frank sustained the Talmud expresses unequivocally the need for Jews to sacrifice Christians. As I have already told you, this was utter nonsense. It is a lie, a horrendous lie. There is not a single page written by a Jewish sage that calls for any kind of human sacrifice, let alone Christian sacrifices. But there is something more I could retrieve from that theological discussion. During it, the fate of a little Christian girl was also discussed, Halina Brunnow. Remember her? I told you about her death. Let me refresh your memory: in 1753, her body was discovered in Zhytomyr, and the locals blamed the Jewish community for her death. This prompted a pogrom that killed almost all of Zhytomyr's Jewish population. So, that is it. You have a link between Jakob Frank and Joseph of Lemberg. Frank was sure that blood libels were true, and you know that a specific blood libel that led to a pogrom happened in the town where Tikvah got its name. I am sure you will know what to do with all this information.

All the best,

Debra

He felt his mind had been blown away. There it was: the bleeding star, hidden in plain sight in some old paintings of even older Jewish sages. Then there were the blood libels and that crazy rabbi, Jakob Frank, who told all those hurtful lies in Lemberg when Joseph of Lemberg would have been a teenager! Could it be that he had been present at the theological debate?

His phone rang. Matt was so focused on the computer screen that he noticed nothing else happening around him. He took the call. It was from Laura. She wanted to come to his place. Matt wasn't feeling very much like seeing her. Still, he also needed some time to think about all the revelations he had just received, so he told her to come by whenever she liked. He stood up and took Bernard Malamud's *The Fixer* from the bookshelf. He went to bed and read it while waiting for Laura.

Something was fascinating and scary about what was going on. Blood libels had always been around. He knew that now. They were just made-up stories forged to push anti-semitism and persecution of Jews. But now, it seemed like they were happening in real life, as if someone had taken those lies and read them as a recipe for murder. But why? Why do that? Apart from the old-as-life antisemitism, he couldn't think of anything.

The buzzer rang. Laura had arrived. Suddenly, his mood changed. He was happy to see her again. And yet, they still had almost nothing in common. He hadn't spoken with her about his investigation and what he was getting into. Would she still look after him if she knew what he was doing?

"Do you want to have Chinese for dinner?" he asked her as they entered his apartment.

"I can cook something for us," Laura offered. That was something new as well.

"Really? I would certainly appreciate it," he said and immediately regretted it. What was that supposed to mean? "Appreciate it"? What was he trying to say?

Laura didn't care about the wording and went straight to the kitchen.

"I don't know if you will find anything you can use to cook with, though," he said.

"Oh, I will manage. Don't worry," she said.

"Perhaps I can help you out."

"Sure, but you will have to follow my lead. Are you up to it?"

"Let's find out."

They cooked parmesan chicken. Matt thought it tasted great.

"I didn't know you could cook."

"There is plenty of me you don't know. Yet."

"Why is so?"

"I don't know. It is just what it is, right?"

"Yes. And you don't know much about me either."

"That is fair. Do you want to share what you are up to?"

"You go first," said Matt while they were having dinner beside the candlelight.

"Fine. Well, maybe I have been a little absent lately. I have been helping my sister put up the new collection for my father's fall collection."

Matt remembered that Laura's father was a prestigious clothes designer. Although to be honest, he had never been much interested in fashion.

"He is having this big event, and my sister has been very involved. He wants her to follow his path once he is retired. And my sister wants me to her side, so I have been doing that for the past few months."

Matt found it fascinating that he had never talked with her about that. He barely knew her and still felt like he was under her spell.

"And what about you?" she asked with what he thought seemed legitimate curiosity.

"Well, honestly, you wouldn't believe what I've been researching for the last few weeks."

"Try me," she said with a provocative smile.

"I..." Matt struggled to come up with a straight answer, even just an answer, when his cell phone started ringing.

"Excuse me, I have to take this call," he told her, taking advantage of the distraction.

He heard a lot of noise, shouts, and honks from the other side of the line. He then heard the voice of a woman.

"You need to come here! You need to take me out of here!" the woman screamed.

"Who? Who are you?"

"This is Shayna! Turn on your TV. Put a news channel or something!"

"What? What is going on?"

"Just turn on the TV, now!"

He looked for the remote control throughout the dining room. He barely used the TV. When he finally reached it, he turned it on. Laura went by his side.

"What is going on?"

He looked up the news channel and saw what Shayan was most likely talking about. A big fire burned down a building that he knew belonged to Tikvah. People were fighting in a riot all around the place.

"You need to come and take me!" repeated Shayna. "Find me. Take me out of here!"

"Where are you?" Matt said, feeling increasingly uneasy.

"I don't know the exact address. It is Tikvah's boarding school for girls. Look for it and meet me here."

The communication ended.

"What was that? What is going on?" asked Laura, annoyed.

"I'm sorry, but we'll have to finish our dinner another day," he said as he searched frantically in the Maps app on his phone for where Shayna had told him to look for her.

CHAPTER 29

ORTEGA

He received a message from *Rubberface* a week later. At last, someone was willing to buy the silver coin. A meeting had been set for the following afternoon. Ortega thought it wouldn't be wise to go with the first person who seemed interested in it. Still, *Rubberface* had convinced him he had turned every stone, and no one seemed to want to get involved. Not only did no one know anything about that strange coin, but the few who had been interested had quickly lost interest when they found out it had something to do with Jews.

"So, who is this guy?" asked Ortega, leaning into *Rubberface*'s desk. The client was set to arrive in half an hour.

"I don't know him, nor have I ever conducted business with this gentleman. He was a referral."

"You got a name, at least?"

"No, no names. I only spoke with the man by phone. He had a thick accent, like German or something."

German? Ortega remembered that the rabbi he had interviewed, Isaac Setzer, also had a German accent. After talking to the man, he discovered that Yiddish, a German dialect or something like that, was many orthodox Jews' mother tongue. So this man was probably one of them.

They waited there all afternoon, but the buyer never showed. Ortega felt frustrated.

"Well, it seems like our guy got cold feet. Why don't you give him a brief call?"

"I don't have his number," said *Rubberface,* with a hint of embarrassment.

"What?"

"This client was very concerned about his privacy. He only agreed to call me from a burner phone and never gave me any other information."

"I can't believe this shit," said Ortega, frustrated. "You acted like an amateur!"

"I am sorry," said the other.

"Yeah, well, call me if he gets back at you, okay?"

"I will surely do that," said *Rubberface.*

Ortega left the bar and walked to the corner where he had parked the car. The sun was coming down, and the sky was gleaming orange. He lit a cigarette and took a few puffs to calm himself.

Then, suddenly, a black car stretched through the street, stopping in front of *Rubberface's* bar. The front companion seat door opened, and a masked guy, wearing black from head to toe, got out with an AR-15 rifle.

"Shit," Ortega mumbled before reaching for his .38

CHAPTER 30

ORTEGA

The man who got out of the car entered the bar. Ortega ran to meet him, only to be greeted by gunfire from the driver's seat as he stood in the middle of the road. He took cover behind another parked car and responded to the fire. It all happened quickly. He could hear screams inside the bar but could not advance. Ortega could barely hold his position as the driver fired an automatic rifle. He was stuck behind the parked car. If he moved forward and tried to get to the attacker's car, he would not have a place to hide and would end up with his body filled with lead. He would blow any cover he had left if he tried to retreat. It was a dead end. A bullet passed through, kissing his left cheek, leaving a painful burning sensation. A close one.

Then, the hooded man who had entered the bar ran and got into the car while the driver covered him with a continuous burst of bullets. The car took off while Ortega kept firing his .38 at it until he ran out of ammunition. Then he heard a broken, sad sound inside *Rubberface*'s bar. He ran inside and went straight to his friend's office through the passageway. There was the woman he had seen the last time watching Mexican TV shows, crying while she held *Rubberface* in her arms. His face was covered in blood, and his eyes were wide open and still. Ortega knew immediately that he was dead. The barman was also there, standing in front of the scene, silent, visibly shocked.

"What are you doing? Call an ambulance!" shouted Ortega while approaching his friend's corpse. The man ran to the front of the bar and went to the phone.

Ortega knew he was ultimately responsible for what had just happened.

"*Mi amor, mi amor, mi amor,*" said the Mexican woman, choking with tears.

Ortega approached her and put a hand on her shoulder.

"Can you tell me what you saw?"

"*Ese hombre,*" she said, "he entered here. It was all so sudden. I was in the other room, only to hear that he asked for a coin. José gave it to him. I am sure because he wouldn't want any trouble. And then I heard the shots. I knew immediately that something terrible had happened. Why, why did it happen?" she cried again.

Ortega felt sorry for the girl. She loved his old pal.

"And then what happened?" he asked her calmly.

"And then, and them *fui a ver qué había pasado*, I went to see. I got out of the room. I crossed this hideous man, wearing all black and a mask."

"So you couldn't get any glimpse of him. You don't know how he looked?"

"*No señor*, he was tall. Very tall and thin. All I saw was that. We crashed into each other in the hallway. I didn't know! I saw him carrying this enormous machine gun, but I didn't know!"

"I understand. So, then, what happened?"

"Then, the man pushed me aside and briefly pointed his gun at me. I screamed, and he ran away."

Ortega looked at the scene. It all seemed like he had left it fifteen minutes ago. It only took fifteen minutes for all hell to break loose. Now, his friend was dead, lying in a pool of blood.

They had taken the coin. Of course, they had. Also, one of those butcher knives he had seen in the slaughterhouse was used to nail a piece of paper to the top of the desk. Ortega took the paper. It had a picture and a clear message:

Jews will work out their differences among themselves.
Pesach is approaching, and we must bake the matzah.

It was the same message as the one found at the scene of the Purim murders.

He heard the sirens of the approaching police cars and wondered, "Now what?"

INTERLUDE

FEBRUARY 20 AND 21, 1753 - OUTSKIRTS OF ZHYTOMYR, POLISH-LITHUANIAN COMMONWEALTH

Joseph felt the cold freeze entering his nostrils and ears. He took a deep breath, exhaled, and sensed how his tears froze on his cheeks before reaching the ground. He had only been hiding there for a short while, but he had the impression that it was the longest time he had ever been exposed to the elements during the dead of winter. He couldn't just figure out how he had escaped the same fate as his family. Years later, he eventually would become convinced it had been nothing short of a miracle. That HaShem had taken him in his hands and hidden him among the bushes, far from the mob's bloodthirsty rage. It had all happened so quickly. He and his family were escaping, and then they suddenly found themselves surrounded by an angry crowd. His mind was blank for what had happened next, just as white as snow. The next thing he knew was that he had been separated from his family, safeguarded in a patch of land that the night had made invisible to the others. He instinctively knew that to survive, he had to keep still and not move. Years later, Joseph would tell himself that the courage he had found that night and the fact that he could blend in with the trees and bushes around him were also part of HaShem's miracle.

His father had taught him that every Jew has to recreate the saga of the Jewish exodus from Egypt during his lifetime, and he was doing just that. It was sad and painful, just like it had been for his ancestors. It had started at that moment and would last for six years, although he didn't know it while watching the blood of his family being spelled in the snow. At that precise moment, he realized he had to run away as fast as he could. The crowd would probably realize he was missing and follow his footprints. He had a slight advantage, a divine advantage, but yet small, and he had to take it. So he ran away from there, leaving what was left of his family to rot in the open. He ran as fast as he could until he was out of air. It was the middle of the night, and he could hear wolves howling nearby. He had to find somewhere to rest until the morning. A big, robust oak tree seemed the best solution. With an enormous effort and gasping for air when he was midway to the top, he finally got into a stable branch a reasonable distance from the ground. He could hear wolves howling in the middle of the night, but he also saw what he had expected: torches breaking through the darkness, heading for him. They went through without noticing him and only turned around when the wolves' wailing howls got too loud.

It was only then that he fell asleep. Horrible, vivid nightmares where he could see again and again his family being slashed populated his dreams until a new, heavy snowfall woke him up. It was dawn, and the horrors from the night before had washed away. There didn't seem, at first, glance, to be any predator or dangerous animal in the surroundings. Still, he was hungry as never before. He had also never spent so much time alone in the forest and was unsure what to do or how to proceed.

He felt his limbs were stiff and about to freeze, so he decided to get down from the tree, look for firewood, build a fire, let his body warm up again, and then try to catch a small animal to eat. When he could move his legs and arms again, he slid to the ground. The trunk of the tree was cold and humid with the new snowfall. His left foot slipped, lost control, and fell into a snow pile that mitigated the pain. He had twisted his ankle, and the pain was intolerable when he tried to get up. Now, his head was also aching, and he had a new feeling that he would die alone and cold. He started crying out loud. It was not the wise thing to do, for sure. With the animal and human predators after him, his loud sobbing would give him away if anyone was nearby, but he didn't care. He thought that maybe dying was not all that bad, considering how things were for him then. The pain, physical and spiritual, was unbearable. And then he fainted. He had new nightmares, now inhabited by the ghost of Halina Brunnow, the baker's daughter. He had known her. She had been his friend. Joseph's mother had been clear that he was not allowed to establish relationships with the goyim, but he still had with Halina. He hadn't planned on developing a relationship with the girl; it had just evolved naturally. One day, Joseph went to town with his mother for errands. He used to help her bring back groceries to their home when he was not studying the Torah. That day, they ended up in the bakery. While Joseph's mother bought the bread, Halina, the baker's little daughter, helped her father. She handed the bread to Joseph, and they exchanged some timid words. The bread the girl had handled him was hot, just taken from the oven. Halina smiled at him, acknowledging the fact, and he felt a sudden blush gaining on his face.

Since then, whenever Joseph's mother needed to go to town for bread, he would volunteer to go with her. He didn't care as much for doing the right thing for his poor mother and his family but for the occasion of getting to meet little Halina.

At first, they only had a few words to say. Joseph was painfully shy, and though the girl was outgoing, her father had cautioned her not to get too close to the Jews.

One day, Halina slipped Joseph a note when their parents weren't around. Joseph felt a sense of vertigo. He waited until returning home and, in a rare moment of not being surrounded by anyone, read the message. Halina had invited him to meet her at the bank of the Teterev River. Joseph ultimately attended the date after giving it some thought. They met on a beautiful, sunny spring day. They found themselves together and away from any controlling adult for the first time since they got to know each other. They were both excited by the vertiginous sensation of knowing they were doing something forbidden. However, that first meeting went painfully awkward as they sat in a fallen tree trunk and said nothing for an hour. Then Joseph announced he needed to get back to his home. Before leaving, he asked Halina if they could repeat the encounter. She doubted for a second because the silence between them had made her think he was not having a good time, but ultimately accepted. They started meeting at the same spot every week and repeated the routine from their first time on each occasion. They would stare at the Teterev and say a few words. They needed nothing else. Being together, although with little talking, was sufficient for them.

Things changed when, one day, Halina proposed to Joseph that they go into the town. He wasn't convinced at first. They practically didn't risk being seen by their parents at the bank of the river. Halina pushed him until she was able to convince him. She told him it would be fun to sneak out through the narrow streets of Zhytomyr and try not to get caught by an adult, which was against the law that said Jews and non-Jews couldn't mix. It made little sense. How could his mother buy bread from his father when they could not spend time together? How did Joseph's mother come to the bakery at the start of spring to sell Halina's father the bread and wheat she had just bought from him a few days before?

The boy also couldn't understand the rule his parents made very clear almost every day: "You should not spend time with the goyim. They don't like us and will never like us." But Halina clearly liked him, and he liked her. So why wasn't he allowed to spend time with her? It made little sense.

On that day, they went to town together. Walking through the city's maze-like streets, no one noticed the young Christian girl and Jewish boy. They had a good time, much better than if they had stayed by the river.

It had poured the previous days, and it took them no time to get completely covered in mud up to their knees. Joseph was thinking about explaining this to his mother when he got home when something unexpected happened: they ran into Halina's father on a side street. All of it happened quickly. A door opened, and the man walked out as the kids walked by. A blonde, middle-aged woman with scrambled hair and wearing worn clothes had opened the door from where Halina's father had appeared. He looked happy and relaxed, and the eyes of the woman were also filled with joy. However, when the baker saw her daughter hanging out with the son of the Jews, all his peace of mind fell off. Halina noticed her father was coming out of the lateral door just when they had passed and grabbed Joseph by his hand. She pushed him and told him to run with her. His father, noticing the situation, ran behind them, shouting insults at the boy.

The children made it out onto a busy street. Taking advantage of their short height, they blended in with the crowd and left behind the agitated baker for a considerable advantage. They got inside a dark alley and ran, looking for a place to hide while the man followed them, closing at every second. Halina told Joseph it was time for them to split, that he should return home, and that she would deal with his father. Knowing the baker would catch them, the boy complied and left, not before asking her if she would be all right. Halina assured him she would defuse his father. She knew how to talk the man into reason.

The next time they saw each other was once again in the bakery. Joseph's mother went to get bread, and he went with her as if nothing had happened. His family did not know he had been meeting Halina behind their backs. On that day, the baker said nothing to Joseph's mother or even looked at the boy. But Halina was severe and quiet, and a blood clot could be seen under her right eye. The second she got away from her father's inquisitive eyes, she passed Joseph a piece of paper, like the time that had started everything. The paper asked him to meet her again that same afternoon at the bank of the Teterev River.

Joseph arrived a few minutes early for the scheduled meeting. He was nervous and could tell that something was wrong. He had a feeling that his friend's blood clot directly resulted from her father catching them together.

It was a sad afternoon for both. When the girl arrived, she went directly to the tree trunk, where they had spent many more joyful afternoons. Joseph immediately knew that his feeling was correct. Something had broken between them. It wasn't the same. There was a palpable sense of loss in the air, he thought. Halina's black eye ruined her perfect little blond face.

"I think we should not see each other again," she said timidly.

Joseph didn't respond. He silently accepted her words and walked back home, giving her his back.

A week later, a pogrom erupted in the town. The crowd accused the Jews of killing the little girl. Joseph felt he was responsible. He had killed her and his own family. He had been told not to talk to non-Jews, but he did it anyway. And now Halina was dead, and his family and his friends and other Jew families that were friends with his family were all dead. HaShem had wanted this to be his punishment for his disobedience.

He woke up feeling a pain he had never felt until then. It was all over his body, and he sensed death approaching. His ankle soared, and he couldn't get to stand up. His entire body was buried in the snow. He would perish in the elements or be devoured by wolves. He accepted his plight as inevitable.

And then, a cheerful whistle came his way and made him look up. Someone was walking his way. That kind of whistle was not one that birds would do, but a human being. If the man were one of his hunters, he would probably die. But if he didn't try reaching him, he would certainly die.

Joseph shouted for help in Yiddish. The whistle he had heard resumed with the same cheerfulness he had noted the first time. Joseph shouted again, crying for help, and a man figure appeared behind the trees near where he was struck. He cried for help once more, and the walker came to him. It was an old man wearing simple clothes, an oversized white tunic that made him almost invisible in contrast with the snow, and a fur hat. Various amulets hung from his neck, carrying a leather bag and a walking stick of a tree branch.

The man came close to Joseph and noticed his sore ankle. Without uttering a single word, he knelt in front of the child. Then, after searching for a balm in his bag, he applied it to the swelling zone while reciting a prayer.

Joseph felt immediate relief. His body recovered heat, he could feel the blood returning to his limbs, and his ankle was relieved of pain.

"Thank you," he said timidly to the man.

The stranger smiled and told him,

"Whoever saves one life saves an entire world," he responded.

Joseph had heard that phrase before. His father used to repeat it to him and his siblings, but it was not until that moment that he could understand it.

"My name is Joseph," he told the stranger.

"I am called Abraham Baal Shem, and I come from Zhovkva, north of Lemberg. I had been in the forest for some months now. I went outside and thought about how HaShem is in everything, and now I'm here." He stopped and smiled. "I suppose you would like to return home. I can help you if you tell me where you live."

"I no longer have a place to call home. Nor family," said Joseph, feeling tears coming down his eyes.

The stranger had heard the news about a pogrom the day before around that area. After giving it a little thought, he told the child,

"You can come with me then."

"And to where?"

"I don't know. Wherever HaShem wants. And then, back to Zhovkva, or if you prefer, I could bring you to Lemberg. You will probably find a substitute family there. If you come with me, I could tell you stories and songs and teach you the secrets of the Kabbalah."

Joseph looked at Baal Shem with distrust. He didn't fully understand that man's motivations, but he had no alternative but to go with him.

"Come on, before it gets too dark," said the man, stretching his hand to the child.

Joseph saw the hand, worn and with long nails, with tiny amulets hanging from his wrist. He had nothing else to lose, so he took the hand and got up. His ankle had stopped hurting. The man had done some magic, no doubt.

"Come with me," said the Baal Shem, and Joseph walked along his side into the forest, leaving behind the scenes of horror and death that would still haunt his conscience for the rest of his life.

CHAPTER 31

SHAYNA

As Pesach quickly approached, Shayna was informed that she would be expected to assist in the preparations. Tikvah's Women's House was going to host a big celebration.

After just one week at the boarding school, her mother began making regular visits. Sometimes, her younger siblings tagged along. During their conversations, Shayna's sins were never spoken out loud. Instead, they used to talk about silly things and gossip about what was happening in Tikvah's community. They also spent a lot of time planning her future wedding. Shayna had lost any interest in the matter. Still, she pretended otherwise so that her mother wouldn't have to endure more pain because of her. Shayna faked her interest in everything about the wedding. She was very good at acting surprised when her mother told her about all her responsibilities as a wife. The aspects of modesty laws, marital responsibilities, and the expectation that she would engage in sexual activity with her husband whenever it was not prohibited presented particular challenges for her mother. Shayna found all that both fascinating and dull. The idea of becoming a slave to the desires of her future husband and the biblical precepts was becoming increasingly frustrating in her mind.

Also, she found the purification ritual at the mikvah a little disgusting. She was to take her first bath in the private pool the day before her marriage. After that, every month for the rest of her life, seven days after her periodical impurity had ended. The idea of taking a private bath in a collective pool filled with rainwater that many other women had already used seemed anti-hygienic to her.

Shayna looked at herself in the mirror. She was wearing a soft white shirt and a long pleated grey skirt that reached her ankles. Her hair was bunched up on top of her head. She saw herself having to wear a ridiculous wig. That was how she was to show her modesty. The wig, the discrete clothing, would demonstrate that she was a private woman, a woman taken by a man, not available to any other man. Then she thought about how her body and belly would grow bigger after each baby she was supposed to have. As many as God sent her. Her belly would deform, she would gain weight, and she would become someone else. In the reflection, she saw herself. Shayna Lehrer was her name. Soon, she would look in the mirror and no longer recognize herself. And that terrified her.

She was becoming aware that something was wrong with her upbringing. Why did Tikvah go to such lengths to ensure everyone in the community followed the rules if they were natural and easy to accept? A table with brochures explaining all those silly rules was placed at the entrance to Tikvah Women's House. For instance, the one that said only a woman's husband could touch her. Not even her sons when they are accepted as men in the community. She remembered how his father, who used to be so close and affectionate with her when she was a little girl, had suddenly stopped kissing her cheeks goodnight when she had become a woman.

She thought about her mother, a defective birthing machine that had to leave everything behind, her dreams, if she ever had them, to accompany his father on his trips around the world; how her mother had to adapt to different times, places, people, weathers; how she and her father had always had to start from the bottom, getting the life only what the rabbi could get in donations for their cause could let them afford. How her mother had to go through all her pregnancies once she had got them. How much more at stake was for her mother because she was married to Rabbi Moshe Lehrer, Tikvah rebbe's right hand. She had to be extra careful not to do nor say anything inadequate; that was not what she was expected to do or say. Even doing everything right and following a perfect Jewish wife's life, she also had to deal with the gossip behind her back. She had to know that people in the community talked to her back about her, her husband, and how complicated her pregnancies had been.

Nevertheless, she could not say or do anything about that. She was always in the spotlight only because she had married one of the most respectable sages from Tikvah. And Shayna knew it was that exact fate she could expect after marrying Mordechai Posner.

Her mind kept racing with these ideas as she continued living the life they expected her to live, helping with the Pesach festivities. She had been put in charge of searching for all the possible remaining chametz in the five-story building, particularly inside the rooms but excluding places where it could have never been, like the temple on the first floor. She was also in charge of checking the chametz-selling forms that many families in the community brought to Rabbi Goldfarb so that they could get his blessing. Every piece of food made of leavened flour had to be sold to non-Jews. As it could be difficult for families who were not used to talking or interacting with the goyim to carry out the selling, Tikvah provided a service of massive sales that was very convenient. Shayna had also helped put foil paper on the kitchen's walls, tables, and burners. She had supervised the *libun gamur*, the kashering of the cookware. She had poured boiling water over pots, pans, and everything in between. Pesach was the most exhausting of the festivities because of its required preparations. Every precaution had to be taken to ensure that not even a breadcrumb remained on the premises. Having been unable to lend her mother a hand this time for the preparations in their family home, Shayna could only imagine how taxing the process had been for her.

She was particularly frustrated with how her life was going, but more with the perspective of living another sixty, maybe more years, where all those things would continue to be part of his everyday routine.

She felt a gentle vibration as she lay on the bed, contemplating all that. Could it be? The phone someone had left at the door of her room the day she arrived was still there with her. She hadn't used it but kept it charged just in case. And now it was vibrating and making sounds. She looked for it, took it from under the bed, and looked at the screen that showed that she had received a text message. She felt her heart racing. She had handled the phone with extra precaution, still convinced it had all been a trap set by her father or maybe Rabbi Goldfarb to test her commitment to Tikvah and the life she was supposed to live. She couldn't resist anymore. She needed to see what that text message was about, even if, by doing so, the door of her room opened, and her father burst inside screaming that she had let him down once again.

She opened the message and read it two times. It only said one word: "Boom!" It made little sense. She searched for the number that had sent the message. "Private number," it said. And then she felt something stumping on the window of the room. She felt the shock as if a pigeon had missed its way and crashed into the window. She got up from the bed and went to see, and then a brick went through, crashing through the window and sparkling broken glass all over. She stood there without knowing where to go or what to do for a second, and then the sound of crashing windows emerged. The Tikvah Women's House was under attack, and she could hear the rage coming from the streets in shouts that urged for the killing of all the Jews. Another brick came in through the window of her bedroom and almost hit her on the head. Orange glimpses of light coming from torches in the streets reflected on the broken glass all over the floor. She felt a paralyzing fear, an ancestral knowledge that this day would eventually come for her; for every Jew in the world.

The bedroom door opened violently. Shayna took her hands to her face. She didn't want to see what was coming for her. Instead, she heard the voice of Shterna Daye:

"Come on, Shayna! We must protect you!"

Shayna looked in the voice's direction and saw the woman still wearing a nightgown. She then took the phone without caring what Shterna would think and followed her to the hallway.

"What is going on?"

"It is a pogrom, dear Shayna. They want to kill us all! We must run and get out of here before they burn the entire building!"

It was all chaos. The fire spread from the empty rooms, and sirens could be heard in the distance, but the shouting almost drowned them out and chanting on the street. Shterna took Shayna by the hand, and they went downstairs. It was chaos of women running all over the place. Shayna could see how, outside, all the men who worked and lived in Tikvah Women's House had formed a human chain to protect it. They were facing a mob carrying torches and chanting, "You will not replace us!"

"Come on!" shouted Shterna to Shayna, taking her opposite direction. They went through the kitchen, and then Shterna stopped.

"Listen, Shayna," she told the girl, "I want you to have this key. You will go to the backdoor and exit through there. Wait for me there. I need to help other people. I will send them your way."

She nodded in silence. The screams and sounds of clashing bodies outside the building reached a new intensity. Shayna took the key that Shterna offered her and ran in the opposite direction, searching for the backdoor. She was filled with anger and fear and also a sense of desperation. She got outside and found herself alone and away from where everything was happening. She sensed she would not be helping much staying there but had promised Shterna that she would do that. Then, a thought got into her head, and she knew she had to try. She took the phone out of the pocket of her dress and called the only number on its list.

Matt's voice came from the other side.

"You need to come here! You need to take me out of here!" she shouted.

CHAPTER 32

MATT, SHAYNA AND ORTEGA

"I need to get out of here, now!" screamed Shayna to Matt when he arrived at her encounter.

"Calm down. Why don't I help you get home?"

"No, no, no, you need to take me with you somewhere safe. Not a police station or my family's home. Somewhere safe."

Matt then took her with him to his apartment. It was still possible to hear the rioters and police clashing, and it was anyone's guess whether the unrest would spread to other parts of the city.

He wasn't sure what to do next. The whole thing had blown out of proportion. This was not a game anymore. He couldn't keep pretending to be the dime novel sleuth. Now, the daughter of a Tikvah rabbi was in his apartment. He needed to call Carlos Ortega. Wasn't he the man Margaret Wainstein had sent to investigate the case instead of him? He called him, and after explaining who he was again to the man, they agreed Ortega would be at his apartment as soon as possible.

Shayna went out of the bathroom. She seemed embarrassed.

"I am sorry if I have caused you trouble," she said upon looking to the dining table where there was still a set of two plates and cups, wine, and candles lit. Laura was gone. He had told her to stay, but she found a quick excuse and left.

"It is fine," he responded, although he knew that was not true. "But may I ask you why you called me? Why did you think of me to come for you instead of... I don't know, anyone else?"

Shayna looked at him in silence.

"What do you mean...?" she finally responded. "I just called the number on the phone."

"Which phone?"

"The cellphone. The one that you left for me in front of my bedroom."

Matt didn't have the slightest clue about what the girl was talking about.

"I am afraid I don't know what you are talking about."

"I see," said Shayna and went mute again.

"So?"

"So what?"

"So want to tell me what is all this about? The attack? The cellphone you think I left in front of your room? I did not know that you were living in that place."

So he hadn't left the phone after all. That confirmed Shayna's suspicion that it all had been a setup by her father or someone working for him. She gave Matt a quick rundown of her whereabouts since they last met in the bar.

"That is why you haven't called me back again," he thought out loud.

"Exactly."

Then he shared the scant information he had gathered about the whole blood libel situation, Sabbatai Zevi, his disciple Jakob Frank, and how it seemed to be a connection with the Tikvah's first rebbe.

"This is amazing work you have done!" said Shayna, excited.

"You are telling me you had no idea about this?"

"Of course not! These aren't things that are talked about inside of Tikvah. I honestly knew nothing about these... things."

They heard the chirp coming from the intercom.

"It is fine. It is Carlos Ortega. He is also working on the case and will help us," said Matt, noting that Shayna had suddenly become tense again.

Matt greeted Ortega warmly and introduced him to Shayna.

"Take a seat, please," he said to his guests.

"So, you too are investigating the crimes?" said Shayna while she tried to determine if she could trust the newcomer.

"Yes, the mother of your brother-in-law sent me."

"I see."

"I called you," said Matt, "because I think you could be of more help than I am in this situation."

"How so?"

Matt told Ortega what had happened that night.

"Well, I am certainly happy that you are doing fine," he said, looking Shayna's way, "but I am not sure how I can help you."

"Maybe call your boss?"

"You mean, Mrs. Wainstein?"

"She would probably know how to help her," said Matt.

"I could try calling her. Certainly."

"But before that," said Shayna, "if you are investigating the case and we are also investigating the case... wouldn't it be wise to share with him what he had gathered, Matt?"

Ortega seemed surprised by that.

"I thought Mrs. Wainstein had relieved you from duty," he said to Matt.

"She did, but I still could gather some interesting information."

"Well, I wouldn't mind if you want to share it with me."

He repeated all that he had told Shayna before he had arrived.

"What is more interesting," he said, "is this thing my former boss at the library found." Matt went looking for the printings of Debra's photographs from the Encyclopedia Judaica. He showed them how the image of the bleeding star could be created by interleaving the portraits of the two Jewish sages.

Ortega inspected the images.

"Well, guys, you might have found something of worth here," he said while looking in his pants pocket for the paper sheet with a similar drawing of the bleeding star left at *Rubberface*'s crime scene. "Look at this," he said.

CHAPTER 33

ORTEGA, MATT, AND SHAYNA

"Are you sure you have seen nothing like this before?" Ortega asked Shayna, pointing to the drawing of the bleeding star.

"Absolutely."

"Not even by chance?"

"Not even by chance. No. This is something as new for me as for you."

"Well, I will make the call to Mrs. Wainstein then," said Ortega, his tone tinged with obvious exasperation.

"Hold on," said Shayna, "I remember a former Tikvah rabbi obsessed with the false-Messiah thing."

In a flash, Ortega recalled pastor Hinojosa's description of the paintings in his church. He looked again at the kid's pictures that finished the star's figure. They were the same that hung on the walls of the Church of the Revived Messiah, but he would withhold that information until hearing what the girl had to say. It might as well be a coincidence, and he had to be extremely careful when dealing with those two amateurs.

"What can you tell us about this rabbi, Shayna?" asked Matt excitedly.

"Not much. I hardly remember him. I was just a kid when he abandoned Tikvah. I once went with my dad to visit this rabbi at his Tikvah House. My father and this rabbi then went to talk in a private room, and I was left outside. That is when I saw the portrait of Jakob Frank! Yes! Now I remember! It hung from the wall. My father went out of that meeting furious. Not much later, this rabbi abandoned Tikvah. I don't know where the rabbi went after that."

"Do you know why your father got so furious that day after meeting with this rabbi?" asked her Ortega.

"No, I never asked, and even if I had, he wouldn't have told me."

"Any chance you remember this rabbi's name, at least?"

"Yes, that one's easy: Chaim Gorovitz."

"Well..." said Ortega, scratching the back of his neck, "this might be a long shot, but whatever. It sure looks like a coincidence."

"What are you suggesting?" asked Matt

"I will visit Chaim Gorovitz, see if he knows something about an inside cult of fake-Messiah adorers inside Tikvah. Maybe he can provide us with some spiritual guidance. He shouldn't be too hard to find."

"Maybe," responded Shayna, "but even if you find him, you will not be able to speak with him today."

"And why is that?"

"Because today's Shabbos. He will not even pick up the phone."

Ortega wasn't expecting that answer.

"Anyway, let me call Mrs. Wainstein to see what she can do for you, and then I will leave."

"No," said Shayna, "I want nothing to do with any Wainstein."

"What do you plan to do, then?"

"I will stay here as long as Matt is fine with that."

Ortega looked at Matt, who nodded.

"I can sleep on the couch."

"If you believe that is for the best ...."

"I do," said Shayna.

"Fine by me. You already have my number, kid. So, if anything comes up, call me. *Llámame.*"

"Certainly."

Ortega left. Shayna and Matt were now alone.

"I don't know what I am going to do. Coming here... was not wise on my part. Staying would only worsen things. But simultaneously, I know I cannot safely return home."

"I still believe you should at least let them know you are fine."

"You wouldn't understand. They would prefer me to be dead than be here, alone with you."

"Then why are you staying?"

"I don't know. There is something about you...."

Matt blushed.

"Don't flatter yourself. It is just that I have seen little of the real world. My whole life has taken place within the boundaries of Tikvah. You need to understand that all this is new for me."

She came closer to him and touched his lips with his fingers.

"This. This contact, I haven't touched a man in my life," she said.

"I..."

"I know. You have a girlfriend, and I am here when I shouldn't be. I will leave now," she told him while approaching him. "I just want to ask you for a favor."

"What is that?" he asked, sensing mixed feelings.

"I want you to kiss me. I want to know what it feels like before settling with one man for the rest of my life."

"I... I don't think that would be appropriate," said Matt, but Shayna didn't care and placed her lips into his. They kissed timidly.

"Thank you for that," said Shayna.

"I will sleep on the couch," replied Matt, stepping back.

Shayna went into bed feeling ashamed.

When dawn broke, she was already gone.

CHAPTER 34

MATT, SHAYNA, AND ORTEGA

M att woke up alone. His thoughts were racing, and Minerva seemed restless as she paced the studio apartment. It was as if she was begging for food, but Matt had made sure she had enough for the day before going to sleep. He knew animals could sense when something was off way before humans. He was thinking about all that had happened the night before when his cell phone rang.

***

Upon leaving Matt's apartment, Shayna walked through the streets of a city where she had lived all her life but still didn't know. She knew his father's house address, her home, but not much else. She got in a taxi.

"I am sorry. I don't have any money. I have been robbed and need to get home," she said, on the edge of tears. Somehow, that was enough to move the cab driver to drive her home without pay. It was just a few blocks, anyway. She thanked the man and entered her father's house.

***

Ortega had spent the night tracking Rabbi Chaim Gorovitz. It hadn't been as simple as he'd hoped, but after a few phone calls, he finally had an address. He drove to the suburbs first thing in the morning. Now, he was inside his car in front of a dull-looking house, similar to the hundreds surrounding it, except it was painted all blue. It certainly contrasted with the hundreds of similar ash-colored houses from the surroundings. And

Ortega was sure that the neighborhood's homeowner association was probably suing over it.

Ortega hated the suburbs. He had spent his first years living in Mexico City and had grown used to the constant traffic, walkable streets, smog, and contact with strangers. That was why he felt at home once he had emigrated to another big city north of the border. There seemed to be people inside the rabbi's house. He was preparing to go outside the car and knock on the door when a tall, grey-bearded man wearing all black from toe to hat went out. It had to be Gorovitz. Ortega went after him.

"Rabbi, rabbi!" he called to the towering figure.

The man turned and questioned Ortega with inquisitive eyes.

"And who are you?"

"My name is Carlos Ortega. I just wanted to ask you a few questions."

"Ah, yes. Ortega. I heard about you. I was expecting a visit, to be honest."

Ortega was surprised. This man knew who he was. He had to be very careful about his next steps.

"So, what do you say? Do you have some spare time to spend with a gentile?"

The rabbi looked around as if he was trying to find out if Ortega was alone or if someone else was waiting nearby.

"I am really in a hurry right now," said Gorovitz.

"Come on; I won't take much of your time."

The rabbi sighed.

"Fine, fine, come inside. It wouldn't be very rabbinical of me not accepting to answer some questions. After all, that is what we are supposed to do."

Gorovitz guided Ortega inside his house and to his office. The rabbi sat beside a pile of books on his desk and invited Ortega to sit as well.

"So, what can I do for you, my friend?"

"I heard you were once a Tikvah Zhytomyr Hasid. Is that right?"

"Yes, that is correct," said the rabbi, undisturbed.

"And may I ask you why you left?"

"I left because my spiritual search took me places that... how can I put it... the governing rabbis in the organization didn't agree with."

"Care to explain a little more?" said Ortega while trying to get a glimpse of the office where they were. Behind Gorovitz was an extensive bookcase full of leather-bound books with Hebrew writing in gold on their spines. There also were some portraits and photos.

He spotted a young Gorovitz accompanied by other people he assumed also were rabbis as they were all dressed the same; there was a photo of the man in front of a tombstone with Hebrew lettering, and then there were other portraits of people. Finally, he recognized a drawing of Tikvah's last leader.

"You would not understand the reasons I left. It concerns theological discussions that I doubt you would even care about. The important thing is that I left. This happened many years ago, and I don't see how it could apply to your investigation. Because you are researching the recent crimes that have shaken Tikvah's community, am I right? Well, I am glad to help as much as I can, but I am afraid there is not much I can say to you," said Gorovitz, who stood from his chair.

"Do you mind if I ask you some more questions?"

Gorovitz could not hide his nuisance.

"What?"

"I recently learned that there are members of Tikvah who adhere to a theological viewpoint that is at odds with the rest of the organization's tenets."

"As I said, it has been many years since I left Tikvah. How should I know?"

In Gorovitz's bookcase, Ortega spotted a portrait of Jakob Frank. It was almost hidden at an upper angle, but he was sure it was him.

"Have you seen something like this before?" he said, showing Gorovitz the bleeding star he had collected from Rubberface's crime scene.

The rabbi looked at the drawing for less than a second.

"Never in my life," he said vehemently. "Is that it? I think I answered all your questions."

"Just one more question," said Ortega

Gorovitz looked annoyed.

"Fine. What is it?"

"Would you care to explain to me, if this is the first time you've seen this drawing, why do you have a picture of Jakob Frank on the highest shelf of your bookcase?"

Gorovitz's face went pale.

***

The house was in absolute silence. Shayna knew that was not a good sign. On any typical day, her siblings would shout, ask her mom for something to eat, or just be annoying little things. Everything was dark except for a soft glow coming from her father's studio. Shayna went straight there, determined to confront the man once again. She found him studying one of the Talmud books on his desk. The rabbi didn't look back at her when she went inside. Instead, he waved his hand to tell her to sit in the guest's chair. After a moment, the rabbi put down his reading guide, straightened his glasses into his face, and said without emotion,

"Ten years ago, I had this same conversation with your sister."

"At least now you remember you had another daughter," said Shayna defiantly.

"Do not interrupt me," said her father with the same calm tone. "I cannot understand what I may have done to deserve this. This utter destruction of my family and the work of my life. HaShem is my witness that I have observed the precepts and made the sacrifices he requires of his chosen people. Like with Abraham, he is testing my faith, giving me yet another daughter that happily opts out of her family and people."

"You never loved me. Like you never loved Chaia."

"I love all the Jews in the world. That includes you and your sister. I love you so much, and I feel so mortified by you taking her path of sin."

Shayna could not hold her tears anymore.

"Why? Why can't you come here and hug me if you love me so much? Why can't you say something nice for once? What have they done to you that has turned you into this horrible shadow of the lovely father I knew when I was a child?"

"I love you, your sister, and all Jews," the rabbi said calmly. "But what you, Chaia, and Abraham have done cannot be tolerated."

"What are you talking about?" Shayna wanted to scream, but she only whispered.

"I am talking about the end of Judaism. I am talking about the fundamentalists. I have failed, daughter. I have failed to stop them. They have been under my nose all this time, and I have failed to spot them."

"Be clear for once in your life!"

"I am talking about the false Messiah! You know what I am talking about! I am talking about the vipers that crawl under our feet! I am talking about the cult of Sabbatai Zevi, Jakob Frank, and the bleeding Maguen David! Don't make a fool out of your old, tired father!"

Shayna did her best to figure out what Rabbi Moshe Lehrer was saying.

"What do the false Messiah and that horrible sign have to do with us? With our family?"

"My blood is cursed," said the rabbi, lost in his thoughts, "my daughters, my brother, all of them. Heretics. Fundamentalists. Followers of the mumblings of a dying man who had seen the most horrible things one can ever see. The last words of a man who had lost his reason."

"Joseph of Lemberg," said Shayna.

"It is time to bury all this once and for all. Those signs, those writings, that embarrassing past. Everything. But instead of doing that, instead of doing what has to be done, you, your sister, my brother, and all the others with you are only making it worse! Hiding in the shadows and only coming out to perform your bloody rituals! Don't you see that by following this path, you will finally destroy all of Judaism? What the gas chambers and the crematoriums could not accomplish, you will. HaShem has punished us all for our sins, like thinking that being a Jew doesn't require any work or sacrifice. He sent the Shoa, and we were nearly wiped out. And with what you're doing right now, you'll help bring our doom. It will all burn in a macabre festival of blood and death!" the rabbi was now shouting, and his face had turned red with heat. "I will not allow you! Do you understand?! You and all the others engaging in these machinations are now expelled from our community. And let's hope this does it, and you stop playing games because you have not yet seen the extent I will go to protect my people. Even if it means going against you, my own blood."

"I... I don't understand what you are saying, Father," said Shayna, choking with tears.

"Don't dare you lie to me!" the old man yelled at her.

"I only wish you could explain to me what is happening."

The rabbi ignored her plea.

"You cannot ask even a great sage for his life to be an example of absolute rectitude," said her father, now also with tears circumscribing his face. He looked older, absolutely depleted of life.

He pointed his index finger at the door.

"Now get away. You are not my daughter anymore," he said, stone-faced.

***

"I don't know what you are talking about."

"We both know that you know exactly what I'm talking about. The *bleeding star*, is that what you call it?" insisted Ortega, pointing to the sketch again.

"I will have to ask you politely to leave. This conversation is over."

"Just tell me why you have a picture of Frank in your office, and I'll stop asking questions."

"I... I don't know what the portrait has to do with all the things you are accusing me of," said Gorovitz, slightly obfuscated.

"I am not accusing you of anything, rabbi. At least yet. I was just wondering about the portrait."

"I see. Well, Frank was an important Jewish sage. So, I don't see why having a portrait of him would be a crime or even related to that drawing you just showed me."

Ortega licked his lips.

"Jakob Frank was a fraud, and a converse who helped many others convert to Christianity. And you know very well how this *bleeding star* is related to his portrait."

"I have now answered your questions, Mr. Ortega, and would appreciate it if you stick to your word and just leave. Now."

"I lied. I won't go until you tell me all you know."

Gorovitz turned red.

"This is inconceivable. I won't answer any more of your questions. What has been happening is something that only concerns us Jews. Have you ever heard of the concept of mesirah? It is when a Jew denounces another Jew to a gentile authority. I will not engage in any of that."

"I know a few tricks that will get you talking," Ortega said, standing up. "It is up to you, rabbi."

Gorovitz saw the Mexican approaching him. His figure was imposing, and they were alone. The man could torture him, even kill him, without anybody hearing anything.

"Fine," said Gorovitz, shuddering, "I will tell you what you want to know."

"You see? Getting on the same page was not that hard."

***

Shayna was utterly lost. She had nowhere to go and nobody to ask for compassion. She walked a few blocks away from her father's house. What now? Matt was the only person she could think of who could help her. He would probably give her some shelter for the day. The next morning, she would look for a better arrangement. Her father couldn't have meant that she could not return. He would probably forgive her. After all, she was the only daughter he had left. Where would she go if not? But, for now, she had to get to Matt's place. He would help her. She had memorized the way from his father's house to Matt's and started running towards there. It was not even that far. The front door was open. Shayna didn't find it suspicious. She went straight up the stairs until she reached Matt's apartment. The door to his apartment was also open, so she went inside. The place was a mess. It was nothing as she remembered from a few hours ago. Things were all over the place; the mattress was on the floor, and piles of trash were everywhere.

"Matt?" she asked, but nobody answered.

Behind her, the door closed suddenly. A gloved hand covered her mouth and made her turn around.

In front of her was a man she had never seen before. He was wearing a white toga, and his hair revolted in his head. Shayna felt tremors all over her body when the man said to her,

"I was asked to tell you 'Shalom, Shayna Lehrer.'"

***

"First, you need to know I am not part of this. Not anymore, not for a long time," said Gorovitz.

"And what precisely would it be the thing you are not part of?"

"The *bleeding star* stuff and all that. Yes, I still find some of Jakob Frank's ideas and provocations fascinating. Still, I don't worship him or am part of the cult."

"The cult?"

"That is the name some people would give it inside Tikvah. The cult of Jakob Frank and Sabbatai Zevi. The *bleeding star* as you referred to them."

"And what does this cult have to do with the killings? And most importantly, who is involved?" said Ortega, trying to hide his anxiety. The dominos were finally falling in place.

"To that second question, I cannot say with certainty. I am also unsure about the killings, but I can assume."

"Explain it to me."

"It has all to do with birth pains. It entails making life for Jews as difficult as possible to induce mass conversion to Christianity."

"Just like happened in the time of Frank and Zevi?" Ortega couldn't believe he was solving a case talking theology with a disgraced rabbi.

"I assume. Yes."

"But... why? Why is this... cult trying to prompt massive conversions?"

"Because of the same reason, every living Jew would; to finally make the Messiah come to Earth. It has been written that the Jewish people will suffer immensely just before he finally comes. Those are the birth pains I have just mentioned. Times of despair, fratricide, pain. And the cult believes they can make that suffering, so the Messiah finally arrives."

"This sounds nuts."

"It is a deeply held theological belief. I assume a gentile would not understand its complexities."

"I didn't intend to offend you, rabbi."

"You didn't."

"And so, who exactly would this Messiah be?"

"Well, most Jews don't know. Some people inside Tikvah believe that their last rebbe was the Messiah and that he will resurrect from his grave one day."

"You are telling me basically that they believe their rebbe is Jesus."

"Something like that. Makes sense why the cult believes conversion to Christianity is necessary to achieve this moment. Right?"

"I think so. I don't know. I honestly think I am beyond understanding all this shit."

"Well, this is all I know."

"Wait a moment. How do you know about the cult?"

"Every high-positioned Tikvah Hasid knows about the cult. It has been entrenched in its theology since the beginning. No one knows exactly who they are or were, but the rumors have always been there. I became interested in them and their theology some time ago and started researching. While I couldn't find the correct gates to let me in, I learned something about Frank, Zevi, and Tikvah's first rebbe. Enough to pick an interest. A theological interest. That is why I was expelled from Tikvah. One can't even be a little interested in the cult without being kicked out of Tikvah. That serious is. And supposedly, the daughter of Rabbi Lehrer was in the cult. That is why she was also expelled."

Ortega had enough information now.

"Thank you for your collaboration, rabbi," he said while he headed to the door.

Gorovitz said nothing, but he showed defeat on his face.

"One last question," said Ortega, stopping before reaching the exit. "You mentioned the cult is trying to trigger the resurrection of Tikvah's rebbe...."

"That is correct."

"And then what?"

"Well, once the Messiah arrives, he would resurrect all the dead and trigger the world's end, of course."

INTERLUDE

FEBRUARY 21, 1753, TO NOVEMBER 20, 1803

T he orphan and the Baal Shem wandered through the forest for six years, settling nowhere for more than a few days. They would arrive in a new town, greet the local Jewish community, and minister to the sick and the weak with songs, joy, and prayers before continuing west towards Zhovkva, Abraham Baal Shem's hometown.

Poor Jews who were hopeless, crazy, or sick would sometimes follow them for a few days until they got tired. Baal Shem was kind but strict. He made his group fear God while he was amazed by the daily miracle of the Creation, which was in everything. During that time, Joseph learned the healing techniques Baal Shem had developed. The old rabbi had recognized his hunger for knowledge and taken him on as an apprentice. When they were on the road, the young boy learned how to heal by using the secret name of God. He also learned how to get rid of evil spirits and call on angels.

The wanderers got to Lemberg in the middle of January 1759. Joseph, who was sixteen then, felt confident in his kabbalistic knowledge after spending the previous six years in the presence of his teacher and spiritual guide.

They settled on the outskirts of town, where they enthusiastically welcomed the city's poor Jewish residents, most of whom were elderly and sick. For a few months, everything went well. Baal Shem even talked with his disciple about establishing a Hasidic court in the city as he got older and his legs had started to fail. Then, one day, sad news reached them: to elevate their social standing, a group of heretic Jews connected to the false prophet Jakob Frank had staged a theological debate with the city's Christian authorities. The news was a bearer of dark times approaching. Baal Shem knew there was nothing positive to expect from the false Messiah's zealots.

Baal Shem and his disciple discussed if they should get involved. They concluded that the best action plan would be to avoid the ridiculous circus Frank's disciples had mounted. However, as the debate date approached, the Baal Shem changed his opinion and told his disciple that he would not want to be anywhere near the town when it happened.

In the dim light of a candle one afternoon, he told Joseph, "I am old now, and the times have come for me to go back to Zhovkva, where I intend to die and be buried alongside my ancestors."

Joseph thought he would once again go along with his teacher. Still, he felt a strange, unknown to him attraction for the theological debate. He knew he could not tell the Baal Shem about this, as it would surely disappoint him. His teacher hated Frank and his acolytes, as he had hated nothing. Joseph was still young and curious, and just as he had accepted the Baal Shem and his teachings, he wanted to learn more about the strange Jews who followed Jakob Frank. He then took a few days to make his decision. Since trusting the man who had saved him from certain death in the middle of the forest, he had never made a more challenging decision. Finally, the young man decided to stay in Lemberg. The Baal Shem felt pride for his disciple. He had taught him all he knew; Joseph could help propagate his teachings around the zone by staying there. Most importantly, he knew that his student would never fall for the lies and deceit of Frank and his cronies, so he accepted Joseph's decision to stay in Lemberg.

Baal Shem's departure was filled with joy and sadness in equal parts. The two men merged in a final affectionate hug and said their goodbyes. They would never see each other again. Joseph was by himself for the first time in the last six years. However, this time was different. He was not a scared boy fleeing a pogrom but a young, promising rabbinical scholar filled with dreams of greatness.

The theological debate went from July 17 to September 10, with days of interruptions. Joseph attended all the instances of the debates. He found the Frankists were unwavering in their beliefs but, in the end, just wanted to find peaceful coexistence with the Christians in town. During the second half of August, rumors poured that Jakob Frank in person was approaching Lemberg to take part in the debate. The fake Messiah arrived on August 27 to his disciples' great fanfare and excitement. He was a small but robust, curved man with tiny incisive eyes, majestic clothes, and a captivating voice. His words spread like a sweet venom throughout Lemberg's Jewish population, including Joseph. It was scandalous and inflammatory, but precisely because of that, the message spread so quickly.

Frank repeated his usual lies in the debate, including that the Talmud requires Jews to sacrifice Christians for Purim and Pesach. Hearing those words coming from an authoritative Jewish figure poisoned the well. Until then, all those horrible lies had been invented, perpetrated, and divulged by envious Christians who wanted to harm the Jews. Now, however, they were coming from a Jewish figure that had garnered attention and respect from his community. Joseph remembered lies like that had cost the lives of his family and, for the first time in years, started crying. He recalled his childhood friend, Halina Brunnow, and how her death had led to the demise of his own family. He saw the images of the blood on the snow, the wolves encircling him, and the night he had spent waiting for death to take him. After hearing Jakob Frank's nonsensical words, he fell ill for three weeks. He spent that time alone in the hut he and his teacher had built on the edge of Lemberg. There, he had time to think in complete silence about the wrongs he had seen and been a part of and the harmful lies of Jakob Frank. He tried to understand why Frank and his followers sought to validate lies that had caused much Jewish suffering.

During the sixteenth night of his retreat, Joseph felt God speaking to his ear and asking him for a sacrifice: he was to sin and to suffer. He was being asked by God to sin and to suffer so that the world could be restored to prepare for the coming of the true Messiah.

That night, Joseph wrote a text that God whispered in his ear. The first words said in Yiddish, "The bleeding star," then it went on: "will rise and shine its light after six generations of sages." The writing contained blasphemies and foretold the Messiah's resurrection after six generations. The Jewish people had to prepare for suffering like what he, Joseph, had gone through as a child. That was the only valid path for re-establishing divinity in the world, just like Jakob Frank had explained the sages of the Talmud required.

During the third week of reclusion, Joseph recovered strength and exited the shack. His pain had been relieved. He attempted to erase what had happened during those weeks. He knew it was a figment of his imagination, a hallucination caused by his sickness and the hurt Jakob Frank's words had caused. The only way to counter all that was the path he knew: joy, happiness, singing songs, and performing miracle cures for the poor. He invited any Jew who wanted to see him into his hut, and it wasn't long before it was full of people who came to sing, pray, and listen to the new Jewish wise man in town. He forgot all about the manuscript he had written during his illness. The papers got lost between all his other papers and books until he completely forgot about them.

The years followed were peaceful and joyful for Joseph, who became known simply as Joseph of Lemberg. He lived modestly, and his teachings continued to bring the attention of more and more people, primarily poor Jews in need from the neighboring area.

By 1763, Joseph had a small reputation and several people who spent all their time with him. His activities were well known by the Jewish community of Lemberg and the surrounding towns. Still, they were mainly a secret for the Christian authorities. This allowed him to continue with his teachings without being bothered by the Gentiles. He was loved by the poor Jews but disliked by the rich, who saw him and his practice as subversive and dangerous.

In 1792, a large group of exiled Hasidim arrived in Lemberg. They were escaping the prohibition of Hasidic kosher sacrifice dictated by Rabbi Tzvi Hirsh Rosanes from Bolekhiv. Joseph decided then it was time to establish his Hasidic court. He had matured during all those years, and now he had a large cohort of people who would follow his teachings. During the next ten years, the Hasidic court grew in power, influence, and acolytes around his figure. By 1802, Joseph's health started to decline rapidly. All kinds of cures were tried on him; benevolent spirits were called to provide him with strength and good health, and help was required from the best kabbalistic sages in the region. Still, nothing seemed to appease the intense pains the now-aging Joseph was experiencing.

On the night of September 20, 1802, knowing that he wouldn't live much longer, Joseph gathered his wife, kin, and closest collaborators. He could momentarily see all he had accomplished and felt happy again. Once all his close people were around him, he told them he hoped to move back to Zhytomyr. He wished to see the place where he had been born and lived during his childhood one last time before dying. He told them that his Hasidic court had to be established there, looking into the future. It would be Tikvah Zhytomyr, and his first-born son, Jakov ben Joseph, would become its next rebbe after his death.

Many tears were shed that night, but a solemn promise was made to him that his last wish would be granted. The next day, the preparations for the journey began. Most of Joseph's followers were poor people with little or no belongings, which made it easier for them to leave their scarce belongings and move along. But Zhytomyr was a long distance from Lemberg by horse. The odyssey took three weeks, given the slow pace they had to go to avoid further upsetting Joseph's health. His body held up well enough to finish the trip, and he could see the land where he had been born so many years before. However, while his body endured enough to survive the trip, his mind did not. Upon arrival, he had almost completely lost what had remained of his sanity. He lived his last days in continuous fever dreams and painful memories of what had happened to his family. On the third day of their arrival to Zhytomyr, he had the worst and most painful fever dream. He saw once again his family being slaughtered, their blood on the snow, and uttered a phrase no one of his followers could comprehend. He babbled his last words and said in Yiddish: "The bleeding star will rise and shine its light." After that, he exhaled his last sigh and died.

CHAPTER 35

ORTEGA AND MATT

Matt sensed something was off and returned to his apartment. He was halfway to a meeting with his brother, his sister-in-law, and their children when he decided to go back. He called Mike and told him something had come up, prompting his brother to call him names. Matt was used to that. When Mike finally finished insulting him, he told him they could meet next Sunday.

"That is a week from now!" screamed Mike on the other side of the line.

"I know," said Matt and hung up.

He rarely sensed things in a paranormal way. But on the rare occasions he did, he had always been right. He had felt wrong one day coming back from school with her mother only to find at their home that there had been a breaking and entering and that they had been robbed. It had also happened to him another time when he was twelve or thirteen years old when he started crying uncontrollably one night because he knew something was off. His mother had tried everything to calm him, to no avail. He just felt that something horrible had happened but could not tell what. His mother informed him and Mike the next day that their grandfather had died in his sleep during the night. She hadn't said anything else, but she and he both knew it was when Matt started crying the night before. And now he had a similar feeling. He felt he needed to return to his apartment because something had happened. Once again, he had been right. The front door was open, and he could see from the outside how his belongings had been scattered all around the place. There were clothes on the floor, his laptop had been smashed against a wall, and even Minerva's cat food had been scattered. He entered the apartment carefully, with cautious steps. He looked for his cell phone, ready to call 911, when he received an incoming call. It was Ortega.

"Hello, kid, I have been digging around this guy your girlfriend told us, and I believe we might be into something...."

"Ortega, good that you called. I am entering my apartment. It is a mess. Someone has been here."

"What? Are you sure?"

"Absolutely,"

"But why? Why you? Is there anything else you haven't told me about your involvement in this case?"

"No, nothing," said Matt while moving through his apartment, trying to assess the damage. It was then that he saw it. It was a piece of blue cloth on the floor.

"Are you still there, kid?"

"Yes. Could you come? I was thinking of calling the police, but there is something I want you to see first."

"Absolutely. Do not call the police until after I arrive."

He hung up.

The piece of blue cloth. Matt recognized it. It was the same color and fabric as the skirt that Shayna wore. He tried to imagine what could have happened there. Why all the mess? It seemed like a fight had taken place there.

"Hello, kid," he heard the voice of Ortega behind his back.

"What? Already here? You almost killed me with a jump scare!"

"When I called you, I was already on my way here."

"What do you think about this?"

"Well, are you sure this isn't how you usually live?"

"This is not funny, Ortega. Someone came here looking for me. And also, look at this," he said, giving the man the blue cloth he had found on the floor.

"This seems to belong to the girl, right?"

"That is what I was thinking. Yes."

"Did she...?"

"Stayed the night? Yes, but don't get any ideas. Before I woke up, she was already gone."

"Well, it seems as if she came back here after."

"But why?"

"I don't know. But when she arrived, someone was waiting."

"They were waiting for me, I assume. And they found her."

"And took her. Not without a fight, judging by what can be seen here."

Matt took back his cell phone and started making a call.

"What are you doing?"

"Calling the police. What else?"

"Stop it right there," said Ortega, taking the phone from his hand. "By the time they arrive, your girlfriend could be dead. We need to finish what we started."

"What are you saying? We still don't know where they could have taken her! We need to call professionals on this!"

"I am a professional kid. And when I called you before, I told you I had some new insights."

"So, what do you have?"

Ortega began to say something and then went completely silent. His face transformed as if he had finally found the missing piece of the puzzle.

"Nevermind. What just happened here is game-changing. There isn't much time left if we want to see your girlfriend live another day."

"She is not my girlfriend!"

"I don't care. Let's split. I have a hunch. I believe I know where they have taken her."

"Well, tell me then! Where did they take her?"

"I don't want to risk it. Let's split. You were going to call the cops. Do that, and I'll see what I can do. I promise to keep you informed if anything arises."

Matt gave it a thought and accepted Ortega's plan. There wasn't much else he could do, and he was eager to call the police on the breaking and entering of his apartment.

***

Ortega got into his car. He took a new look at his notepad and read his annotations. There it was, the Revived Messiah church. He remembered his poor friend, *Rubberface,* who had died because of all this. He owed his old pal the solving of the case.

That motherfucking pastor Hinojosa. He had made it clear about their beliefs with paintings of Jakob Frank and Tikvah's spiritual leader on the church walls. And now, after his talk with Gorovitz, all the pieces seemed to fall into place. He couldn't be entirely sure, but he had to risk it. The life of the poor young girl was at stake. If she was still alive, which Ortega felt was not the most probable scenario. He started the engine of the car and drove to the *barrio.*

***

Matt couldn't stay quiet. He was going through his studio apartment, trying to think clearly but was too nervous. He had called the police and was waiting for them to arrive and, in the meantime, had also looked for Minerva. He had found the poor animal under his bed. She was terrified, and Matt lamented she couldn't tell what her eyes had seen during the past hour.

His cell phone rang, and he hastened to answer, but the communication ended before he could press the button to accept the call. The caller ID said, "Shayna." He tried frantically to call her back, but her phone had been turned off. He looked at his phone screen filled with impotence when he received the notification of a new voicemail message. He listened:

"We got the girl. If you want to see her alive again, come alone. You will find the path," said a distorted voice before giving an address.

He called Ortega, but the man didn't answer his phone. The cops would arrive at his apartment any minute now, but he decided he owed Shayna to try his best to help her get out of what she had fallen into. So he went out, stopped a taxi, and showed the driver the address he had been given.

"That is in the middle of *el barrio*. Aren't you too white-skinned to go there alone?"

"I don't have a choice," he said as the driver took off.

***

Ortega arrived at the Church of the Revived Messiah. The parking lot was empty. He left his car near the entrance in case he had to get off quickly. There was not a single soul to be seen there, which was weird, considering it was Sunday at noon. He had expected people leaving mass, parked cars, and lots of movement. Instead, it was all quiet and tense. He drew his .38 and went out. He walked to the door. It was open from side to side, but the lights were out inside. He cautiously entered with the revolver pointing to his front. He heard a noise to his left side and tried moving his body in that direction, but it was too late. He now had a gun pointing at his head.

"I have been waiting for this reunion," said a voice in the darkness.

"I see you no longer trust your ability to cut my throat."

"We all learn from our mistakes. I wanted to ensure you won't escape your fate this time," said Isaac Setzer.

***

Matt got out of the cab at the intersection of two empty avenues. That was the direction the distorted voice had given him. But what now? There was almost nothing to see there. The location seemed to be far from anywhere. The only thing visible from where he was standing was a parking lot surrounded by empty, abandoned stores and a big mega Church on the corner. It was the only building that had its lights turned on. He walked a few steps through the empty mall parking until he noticed Ortega's car beside the church. He ran toward the car and checked it from the outside. It was empty, meaning that Ortega was probably inside.

He followed through. The lights were on, as he had noticed before, but it seemed like nobody was there. Instead, there were lines of empty chairs, a dais with a podium standing near the opposite end of the building, and a red curtain hanging behind. He walked through the chairs until he reached the podium holding a big, heavy-looking book. He went through its pages. It was written in Hebrew, and he was almost sure it was a siddur, a prayer book. He had noticed the paintings of Christian saints on the walls and then noticed that there was also a painting of Jakob Frank and another of Joseph of Lemberg. He now understood why Ortega had come here. But where was he now? A terrible idea came to his mind. He remembered the crime scene of Purim. He knew these people, whoever they were, liked the spectacle. Shivers went through his body. He had to take down the red curtain. He inhaled deeply and pulled the curtain that fell to the floor. There it was. A big, human-sized wooden cross holding Shayna, who was tied up by her wrists and ankles to it. A rag covered the girl's mouth, and she seemed asleep. He saw Carlos Ortega asleep beside the cross and bound by a yellow flag with a *bleeding star*, the symbol of all that horror. He then felt a cold puncture on his back.

"Turn over to me slowly. Try nothing funny, or I will fill you with lead," said a voice behind him.

CHAPTER 36

ORTEGA, MATT, AND SHAYNA

Matt complied and turned to the man holding a knife against his back.

"Let the girl go," he said, feeling like the situation was unreal.

"In time, we all will be free," said Isaac Setzer.

"Why are you doing this?"

"Shut up. We were waiting for you."

Then Salvador Hinojosa appeared as if he had materialized from thin air. He had been watching the situation unfold from the sidelines.

"Are we ready?" asked Setzer.

"We are," answered the pastor.

"Ready for what?"

"Fine, everyone here deserves to know what is happening. After all, I am a rabbi, a teacher, and I will gladly teach you how important your sacrifice will be for the good of all humanity. First, we will extract the rabbi's daughter's blood. With it, we will knead our unleavened bread like our ancestors ate when they escaped Egypt."

"You are completely insane!" said Matt, unable to contain himself.

"Just listen, will you? You asked, now I am explaining to you. Wasn't that what you asked for?" said Isaac Setzer while unveiling a sacrificial knife he had been hiding inside his overcoat.

Hinojosa pushed Matt toward a side of the wooden cross opposite where Ortega was lying.

"It will be a sacrifice. Bleeding the little princess, Shayna Lehrer," he brandished the knife, "will be painful, and her sacrifice will remind us of the pain our ancestors endured on their journey to the Promised Land. But it will be necessary. Because she has sinned, and with her sins, she has broken the pact between God and his people. That is why she needs to die as our Lord and Savior Jesus Christ also died to purge the sins of humanity.

And when we finally taste the matzo kneaded with her blood, we will enter the messianic times. Then, the Messiah will arrive and rebuild the Sacred Temple of Jerusalem."

"My people, I am going to open your graves and bring you up from them; I will bring you back to the land of Israel. Then you, my people, will know I am the Lord when I open your graves and bring you up from them. I will put my Spirit in you, and you will live, and I will settle you in your own land. Then you will know that I, the Lord, have spoken, and I have done it, declares the Lord," said from memory pastor Hinojosa. "Ezekiel 37:12- 14," he continued.

"This is bullshit," said Matt. "Nobody needs to die for this!"

"But yes, it is needed. The sacrifices are needed. You need to die. Shayna Lehrer needs to die. The Mexican needs to die. This will be the last piece of the puzzle. We knew it. When the last Tikvah rebbe died, we knew it. He was the sixth generation of sages since Joseph of Lemberg. For most of history, the *Bleeding Star* has belonged to the shadows. Now, it is our time to shine and fulfill the prophecy."

The pastor put a pill in Matt's mouth and forced him to swallow it. "Don't worry," said the pastor, "it is just a little something so that you can fall asleep as your friends. You don't need to see what is going to happen next."

Matt felt his body shutting down as he fell to the floor.

Isaac Setzer went to the podium, searched the Siddur, and started reading aloud.

"Isaac!" a sound voice sounded inside the Church. Setzer stopped the reading and looked up. "I finally find you!" completed the voice from the door. It belonged to Shayna's fiancé, Mordechai Posner.

Rabbi Setzer looked surprised.

"Mordechai, we weren't expecting you here just yet."

"And you thought I would miss this moment? Are you guys insane?" he walked toward the dais.

"I thought you had told me he would take care of old man Lehrer so that the *Bleeding Star* could take control of Tikvah," said Hinojosa reproachfully to Setzer.

"I thought the same. So, I assume it is done, right?"

"Calm down. Everything is under my control," said Mordechai Posner, reaching the podium. "Please, pastor, could you take my overcoat? It is hot here," he said, giving it to Hinojosa. The pastor took it.

"Thank you. Can you come a little closer?" said Mordechai Posner to Hinojosa.

"What is all this about, Mordechai?" asked Isaac Setzer, visibly nervous.

"Calm down, my friend! I just want to tell our friend a secret. We have waited six hundred years for this moment, and you cannot wait a few more seconds while I tell Salvador something?"

"Go ahead," said Isaac Setzer with resignation.

Hinojosa leaned toward Mordechai Posner and heard these words,

"Did you think we would be fine with embracing the ultimate sacrifice along a goy like you?"

Salvador Hinojosa had just a second to comprehend the words from Mordechai Posner before being shot in the head. His corpse fell to the floor in a splattered pond of brains and blood.

"Was the theatre necessary?" asked Setzer.

"It had to be done, and now it is done. That is all that matters," said Mordechai Posner.

"Take him away."

Mordechai was pointing his gun at Isaac Setzer.

"What are you doing? Stop that!"

"What am I doing? Do you mean me pointing my gun at you? Just to where your heart is?"

"Stop playing games and put that gun down, Mordechai," said Setzer.

"I am honestly asking for your own good," answered Mordechai Posner. "Do you prefer a single shot to the heart? It would kill you right away, and even though there would be a lot of blood, I wouldn't have to deal with all the brains like this poor scumbag," he said as he kicked the pastor's dead body.

"Cut it. We have more important things to do."

"No, Isaac, this is not a joke. Think about it! If I make just one hole in your heart, it will be easier for the Messiah to bring you back to life after the ultimate sacrifice than if he has to rewire your brain." He walked up to where Isaac Setzer was still standing on the podium.

"Why are you doing this?"

"Don't worry! You will revive like the rest! It will be just a few minutes!"

Isaac Setzer was sweating.

"This is not how we planned all this."

"I know, but to be honest, you never were as clever as you think you are. I have always been the smart one."

"Calm down," said Isaac, trying to reach with the tip of his fingers the gun pointed at him.

"I am sorry, Isaac. The prophecy is clear that only one true sage can stand before fulfilling the sacrifice." Then he fired a bullet through Setzer's chest. The rabbi's face turned for less than a second into a mixture of surprise, pain, and rage before his dead body reached the floor just next to the pastor's corpse.

Mordechai Posner took his place on the podium and, turning to see Shayna, Matt, and Ortega, he said,

"Shayna. My dear Shayna Lehrer. Old Moshe Lehrer's Queen Esther. If you could only gasp the honor for you and your family for being the ones that will finally bring humanity's redemption! If you could only have seen how your sister Chaia embraced the *Bleeding Star* cause as her own! Let's not waste any more time and finish what must be done.

He started reading the Siddur and chanting prayers.

***

It was the second shot that woke up Ortega. He couldn't let that be the end. And he now had an opportunity. Mordechai Posner was praying like possessed, his body aching, moving forward and backward while still standing in the same place. He struggled with the ropes tying his hands until they became loose. He put them on the floor and moved silently toward Shayna. She was still asleep but recovered consciousness after a few soft touches on her face. Ortega asked her to remain silent with a gesture and untied her. When he thought he was finished, he felt a sharp pain in the back of his head. It was the tranquilizer that was coming back. He saw Shayna one last time before falling asleep again. The girl also seemed to lose consciousness again. Then all went black.

***

Matt heard the chanting in his ears. It crept into his dreams to where he realized he was dreaming. He had to wake up, but he couldn't.

Maybe he had been shot, and now, as the rabbi said, he was coming back to life. It wasn't that. He could finally open his eyes. He saw Mordechai Posner's back. He was curved and balancing his body back and forth while chanting prayers. He put his hands on the floor and struggled to stand. He saw Isaac Setzer and Salvador Hinojosa's corpses just beside him. What had happened? It didn't matter now. He looked at Shayna and then Ortega.

They were both still asleep. Their lives now relied on him. He knew he had a chance in Posner praying like a possessed. He didn't see him sneak up behind him. He jumped and tackled the rabbi with his last energy when he was just behind him. They both rolled through the floor. The rabbi's gun sailed a safe distance from them both. They wrestled for a while, but Matt's energy was fading, and he was starting to nod off again. Mordechai Posner sensed it, too, and with one quick move, he dominated him and got on top.

"You will not ruin my sacred mission!" screamed Mordechai, reaching for his gun. He stood up and pointed it at Matt's head.

***

Matt knew this was the end of the road. He had tried and failed. He then closed his eyes and prepared himself to hear the cold kiss of Death on his forehead. Instead, he heard a sticky noise just before feeling the weight of a dead body falling into him. He opened his eyes and saw the corpse of Mordechai Posner. His neck had a cut down the middle from which blood was flowing. Standing beside them was Shayna, covered in blood. She stared at him, her trembling hand clutching Setzer's sacrificial knife.

Matt pushed the dead body away and tried to stand up, to no avail. Shayna extended her other hand and helped him stand. Her eyes were still and looked like they were coming from her eye sockets.

"How do you feel?"

"Not fine at all," she said.

Matt hugged her. For a second, Shayna felt the necessity of pushing him away. She dropped the idea and gave him another hug.

"I killed a man," she said. "I killed my fiancée."

"It was him or us," said Matt.

Shayna seemed not to hear him.

They heard a shriek and immediately looked in its direction. It was Ortega who was recovering his consciousness once again.

"Come on, he needs us," said Matt.

Shayna opened his hand and let the knife fall to the floor. Ortega was sitting on the floor, trying to figure out what had happened.

EPILOGUE

"Excellent job, Ortega," said Margaret Wainstein, extending the man a cheque. "I included a little extra for your trouble."

"Thank you, madame," said Ortega, putting the cheque in his pocket.

"I have been thinking about going on vacation for a few months. Now that my son's case is closed, I thought about maybe going to Italy and then continuing to the East. I don't know how long I would be away, but not less than six or eight months. So I wanted to ask if you would like to come and continue working for me overseas. I mean, I will probably need a driver there as well."

Ortega thought about the perspective of going to Europe for a few seconds. He didn't find it very interesting and was also considering starting his own business. His involvement with the Jews had given him the adrenaline rush he craved from his old days as a police officer in the Policía Federal Preventiva of Mexico. The departure for some months from Ms. Wainstein could allow him to see how well he could do on his own for a change.

"If you do not mind, I would prefer to remain here. I have unresolved personal matters to which I'd like to attend."

"Perfect then. I only hope that I can count on you upon my return."

"I hope so, madame."

He spent the first week of unemployment pretty bored, alone in his office. By the start of the second week, he got a first case as a private eye, and after that, he got more jobs. They were simple and not very interesting. Debt recollection, infidelities, nothing that could excite him like the case he had been recently involved in. When a month had passed, he was referred to work as the fixer for a guy south of the border in Ciudad Juárez. He accepted out of sheer boredom and because he liked the border. He had expected things to be saltier down there, but he couldn't be prepared for what was coming his way.

***

"If you are not good for yourself, you are not good for others," said Shayna.

"What does that mean?"

"Nevermind. It is a Yiddish proverb."

She was sitting beside Matt on a bench under a tree. They were in a park near his apartment.

"Why did you say that?"

"Sometimes, when I feel lost, I find solace in repeating some old words of wisdom to myself. I don't know why. It is just something that comforts me."

They both went silent. Matt kept thinking about everything that had happened. How close he had been to dying inside that church and how Shayna had sliced the throat of Mordechai Posner.

"So, what now?"

"What do you mean?"

"I mean," he said, grasping, "how do we go on? I mean, can we still be... friends?"

"I don't know. Maybe."

"I like you, Shayna."

"I know that. And I like you as well. But I think you like me in a way that...."

"You are just not into me."

"No, not that. It is that you and me... we belong to different worlds."

"I know. And still..."

"Now you see? I am not good for myself. I cannot be good to you."

"Don't try that with me."

"Try what?"

"Finding refuge in an old saying."

"Nothing is ever definitive."

"But you are going back to the herd."

"Maybe. I am not sure yet."

"After all that happened."

Shayna smirked awkwardly.

"I am not sure about my future. I only know that my family and father need me now."

"It thought he had expelled you from Tikvah."

"He has accepted me back."

"And just like that, you are accepting his mild apology. As if nothing had happened."

"I know well what happened and what he did. But he is also an old man who has already lost a daughter. He grew up in a different time, with different ideas. If I want to become an agent of positive change inside my community, I must not leave them now that they need me the most."

Matt was feeling frustrated.

"Your father was almost responsible for your death as well."

"Something happened that I haven't told you. After the events in the church, he reached out to me. And he hugged me for the first time since I was a little girl. And he cried and asked me for forgiveness. He supplicated. I understood what he had done and the logic of his actions. He is a failed man, just like any of us. But at least he could see what he had done wrong and ask for forgiveness. He didn't do that with my sister. Maybe he didn't know how to do it, but he learned a lesson with me, and that is all that matters to me now."

"So, what is next?"

"He is trying to reorganize Tikvah Zhytomyr and clear its name. He wants to clarify that the *Bleeding Star* was a heretic aberration that had nothing to do with true Judaism. It is going to require enormous amounts of energy and will. He will need as much help as he can get."

They went silent once again. Matt looked at her eyes, and she looked back at him. She smiled. They got closer until their lips clashed. They kissed softly first, then with passion. Shayna stopped abruptly.

"I am sorry. I can't," she said and got up.

"This is it, then?" he asked. He didn't want to know the answer.

"At least for now, yes," said Shayna. "However, there is another Yiddish proverb that I would like to tell you."

"Go on."

"It says that one cannot topple a tree with a single blast."

"And what does that mean?"

Shayna smiled.

THE END

THE STORY AND CHARACTERS OF THIS NOVEL WILL BE BACK IN "TEAR RITUALS," PART II OF THE RITUALS SAGA.

FINAL WORDS

*B*lood Rituals is a work of fiction. The characters, situations, and places where the action occurs are fictitious and a product of imagination.

However, some of the historical facts and characters in this novel are true: Baal Shem Tov established Hasidism as a genuine Jewish theology. There is no Tikvah Zhytomyr, although Zhytomyr and Lemberg were once home to large Hasidic populations.

The historical figures mentioned, including Jacob Frank and Sabbatai Zevi, were real people. After the famous Lemberg trial, Frank and his followers converted to Christianity, causing a schism in Judaism. Frank argued that the blood libels were an accurate thing during the trial.

The story about the Ger rebbe, Menachem Mendel of Kotzk, is also part of Hasidic folklore.

Pogroms resulted from accusations of blood libels that were made in Zhytomyr. I could not locate evidence of one occurring in the city in 1753.

The literary works mentioned in this novel by Bernard Malamud, Gustavo Adolfo Becquer, Lope de Vega, and Chaucer are all real and refer to blood libels.

The rest, as they say, is fiction, although sometimes inspired by real facts and characters.

A.J. Soifer

Toronto, Ontario

July, 2023

ABOUT THE AUTHOR

A.J. Soifer lives and work in Toronto, Canada.

He received a Ph.D. in Latin American Literature from the University of Toronto.

OTHER TITLES IN THE RITUALS SERIES

Published

Blood Rituals (Rituals series #1)

Coming soon!

Blood Trails (Rituals series #2)

Tears Rituals (Rituals series #3)

The Way of the Inka (Rituals series #4)

Rituals of Death (Rituals series #5)

EXCERPT FROM BLOOD TRAILS

CHAPTER 1 - THE SMITH & WESSON

Nothing makes you want to reconsider a job as much as to having the barrel of a .38 special pointing directly at your head.

The night was supposed to be quiet, but yet there I was with an upset drug addict in his underwear pointing a gun at my skull. He shouts at me and spits as he does it, his arm shaking nervously, his bare and hairy chest showing all the possible animalistic characteristics that a human can have. His back is arched, his hair covers his face, his brow is furrowed with a furious expression, his eyes are bloodshot, and his underwear is ripped and dirty. His white socks are black with dirt after stepping in the wet grass.

The girl is inside, by the other side of the window. She also screams. She covers her naked body under sheets that don't conceal her well-shaped curves.

If this guy had known how to keep his impulses inside of his pants, we wouldn't be here, and killing him wouldn't be necessary. The last thing I imagined when I accepted working for Walter "The Inka" Ayala was that I would end up in the garden of a modest house of the suburbs, with a drugged and semi-naked rock musician threatening me with a 6-bullet Smith & Wesson Model 19 in .38 Special.

It's a reliable revolver, classic, not too large, but it guarantees the feeling of power to the bearer and it never lets you down.

The guy is sentimental because he prefers an old, reliable, obsolete revolver rather than an efficient semi-automatic pistol that carries out all the dirty work for you.

This jerk made two mistakes: he slept with my boss's wife, and he's pointing at me with a gun.

That's why I'm going to kill him. Images from the night: a worn down bar full of melancholic drunkards and an occasional troublemaker; a rock band at which the guy that is pointing his gun at me and shouting sang some heartbroken and depressing ballads, a couple of tables around the stage and Lucía, the brunette that now is crying behind the window, covering her breasts with the sheets spread on the bed, having a drink and listening, nodding with pleasure by the sound of music; she's the only one interested in the sad laments and groans coming from the band's guitar.

If I were on the opposite side holding the .38, I'd probably also feel I had the situation under control. But this mommy's boy doesn't know me, he doesn't know what Carlos Ortega, Walter Ayala's new bodyguard, is capable of.

So I calm down. It's easy to find out when someone has never shot any other human before: his pulse is quivery, his body moves to the rhythm of his nerves, sweat runs down his face, and his voice trembles. A person that has never killed another human prefers to threaten rather than pull the trigger. If the person threatening you has a higher chance of losing, he's less likely to stuff you with a piece of lead straight in the heart.

This guy has everything to lose.

This little house is simple but picturesque, set in a quiet residential neighborhood with access to the city. It is the fruit of a life of hard work and sacrifice; his rock band, his friends, his short period of working class, and his fans that drag themselves to his bed like serpents of a single night. Like Lucía.

With the exception that this asshole surely doesn't know who Lucía really is. Why would he waste all that for a guy that snuck into his garden with a camera, and took some quick pictures of when he was having a quick fling he'd forget the next morning, in the light of his hangover? Too much to lose.

"I'm working, don't get like that."

"Give me the camera!"

"I'm going to sell the pictures."

He's about to shoot.

"To an entertaining magazine."

He relaxes slightly.

I am a mercenary, that's not a lie.

"You're not going to fool me. Give me the camera."

"I can't."

He's shaking. He hesitates. I could finish this right now, but I still need the girl. And the photos, obviously. I need to show Wally Ayala that his girlfriend has been sleeping with this guy. I don't make any question, I only execute. Lucía was dating the Inka when I started to work for him, and I had only seen her from a distance twice, and then I stopped seeing her all together.

But above all, I didn't ask because I know that not asking questions is the best way to keep you alive for one more night, and then another one, until someday destiny will decide he's bored with us. So tonight, the Peruvian ordered me to follow her. He suspected she was with another man and asked me to confirm it.

I know how to do this job. I've done it hundreds of times in the last year. There are hardly ever any surprises. There is no such thing as "the suspicion of infidelity". There is certainty and the need for disbelief.

"Let's make it simple. Put the gun down, I leave your property, and we forget about the whole thing."

He looks everywhere. The paranoid phase starts in after the rush fades.

"Come on, let's just leave it like this."

"Shut up" he screams.

The girl cries louder. Lucía. She's a beautiful woman, and I would like for her not to be here, in this situation. She knows Inka Ayala well enough to know what's going to happen.

Then I see the .38 shaking fast in the trembling hand of Charly Brun. To underestimate a situation is the mistake that takes most lives from the people working in this business. And at this moment, I feel the situation beginning to slip through my fingers.

Control. I have to do something.

"Why don't we all calm down a little? Let's talk quietly, let me inside your house, we sit down, I show you the pictures I took..."

He hesitates.

"Are you going to erase the pictures?"

"The ones you tell me to."

"Show me."

"Let's go inside and I'll show them to you quietly."

He doubts again. He thinks that in his territory, in his house, he can have a better control.

"Come in," he tells me, all this time keeping the gun trained on me.

I go through the door with my arms raised. Lucía runs into the living room, wrapped up in sheets.

"What are you doing? Why did you let him in?"

"SHUT UP" he shouts to her.

Lucía rushes towards him.

"Are you crazy? Do you know who he is? He works for Ayala."

The guy slaps her face with the back of the hand that is holding the .38. The girl falls to the ground with a thread of blood cutting across the corner of her mouth.

Lucía. You're so beautiful, Lucía. The sheet covering her is a dirty and wrinkled rag. Her eyes are two jade gemstones in the middle of black spots caused by the cheap mascara spread by tears and sweat. I turn on the camera and hand it to the guy.

He reviews the pictures. Charly Brun at his best moment; his best performance. The .38 special is no longer aimed at me; it's pointing at the ceiling.

His expression changes at the exact moment he realizes now I am the one who is pointing at him with a Browning Hi-Power Mark III of 9 mm. I am sentimental, but when it comes to trusting my life to a gun, I prefer the cold precision of a semi-automatic Belgium.

I shoot. A bullet flies directly to his chest. He falls on his back.

Lucía screams. I place my index finger on my lips to shut her up. She cries. She drags herself naked on the floor. The guy is still shaking on the floor, in a pool of his own blood. It looks as if he was drunk and fell on the floor, spilling a bottle of Malbec, but no. It's his blood, and he's dying. His chest goes up and down, trying desperately to keep breathing. His eyes beg for a last moment of mercy, clemency, and he tries to say something. He opens his mouth. He spits blood. I stand next to him. "Amateur," I say and shoot him in the head.